D0971712

GOBBLED BY GHORKS

By Robert Paul Weston

A
CREATURE
DEPARTMENT
Novel

**razOr
bill**

An Imprint of Penguin Group (USA)

razOr bill

A division of Penguin Young Readers Group
Published by the Penguin Group
Penguin Group (USA) LLC
345 Hudson Street
New York, New York 10014

USA / Canada / UK / Ireland / Australia / New Zealand / India / South Africa / China
Penguin.com
A Penguin Random House Company

ISBN: 978-1-59514-750-9

CIP Data is available.   *55468655*
12/14

Printed in the United States of America

1 3 5 7 9 10 8 6 4 2

FOR MACHIKO

CHAPTER 1

In which Harrumphrey goes surfing, Patti takes a breath of brilliance, and Jean-Remy receives a letter

E lliot and Leslie rushed past a green Egyptian pyramid, a green rocket ship, and a green rhinoceros. Does that sound strange? Don't worry. These were perfectly normal things to see—in the courtyard of DENKi-3000. Pyramids, rockets, and rhinos were just a few of the elaborate topiary sculptures carved into the trees and bushes. Most people would have marveled at their grandeur and detail, but not Elliot and Leslie. To them, a privet monkey doing a headstand atop the handlebars of a yew-tree motorcycle was as ordinary as sliced bread. Besides, they were headed for a place much stranger than a few oddly trimmed hedges. They were on their way to the Creature Department.

The tumbledown mansion at the heart of DENKi-3000 rose up to greet them. A tiny figure perched elegantly atop the highest gable.

"Is that who I think it is?" asked Leslie.

"Ah! *Bienvenue, mes amis!*" cried the fairy-bat, Jean-Remy Chevalier.

"Yep, that's him," said Elliot. "But what is he wearing?"

The fairy-bat launched himself into the air and swooped down to hover in front of the children. He was dressed in a skin-tight, one-piece bodysuit featuring thick black-and-white bars.

"*Zees?*" he asked, looking down admiringly at his tiny body. "Why, it is my swimming costume, of course!"

"Swimming?" asked Elliot. "Why do you need a—"

Before Jean-Remy could answer, the front wall of the door-less building split open with a *KERR-RACK*, revealing its secret entrance. Standing on the threshold was Elliot's uncle, Professor Archimedes von Doppler.

"Excellent," he said. "You're just in time! We are in *serious* need of some new ideas!"

The professor waved them into the Creature Department, Jean-Remy flapping above their heads. The secret entrance rumbled closed behind them like the mouth of a monstrous brick-and-clapboard beast.

"Is anyone going to explain why Jean-Remy is wearing a swimsuit?" asked Elliot.

"No need to explain," said the professor. "We can *show* you."

He threw open the doors of the laboratory. Towering in the middle of the huge space, dwarfing the tables and equipment that surrounded it, was an enormous hot tub! The exterior had the raw, unfinished appearance of most things in the Creature Department. The outer bowl was a patchwork of rusty iron sheets, flashing with buttons, switches, and digital readouts. Snaking out from the base were coils of corrugated tubing, all of them juddering quietly, pumping mysterious fluids in and out of the tub.

"This," said the professor, "is the Think Tank!"

He led them up to a large wooden platform that resembled

the patio at a tropical resort. There were deck chairs, colorful umbrellas, and plastic recliners in which all kinds of creatures wore sunglasses and sipped from fruit-filled cocktail glasses (which also sported colorful umbrellas).

The tub was filled with what appeared to be a bright-orange bubble bath. It was big enough to accommodate twenty or thirty of even the largest creatures. Every so often, huge tangerine bubbles, each one as big as a basketball, broke free from the surface and floated high into the air before popping with an audible *THUP!*

On the far side of the tub, Harrumphrey Grouseman, the professor's "right-hand head," floated on a sky-blue surfboard. He had a snorkel and diving mask strapped around his enormous noggin. Hugging his waist (which was basically just below his chin) was a pink inflatable inner tube shaped like the Loch Ness monster. A wave on the surface of the bubbly brew swelled up dramatically, cresting white and pushing him toward the deck.

"Cowabunga," he grumbled.

FWOOSH!

Harrumphrey crashed into the deck, rolling across the planks like a big bearded bowling ball.

"Did you get anything?" the professor asked, helping extract Harrumphrey from the tangle of umbrellas and chairs he had toppled.

"Nothing useful," Harrumphrey answered.

"Get any *what*?" asked Leslie.

"Ideas." Harrumphrey waddled over to join the children by the edge of the tub. His pink Loch Ness inner tube squeaked with every step. "I was surfing a Brain Wave."

"Of course you were," said Leslie (very little in the Creature Department surprised her anymore).

"What is this stuff?" Elliot asked. He leaned over and scooped up a handful of orange foam. "Smells like lemons."

"Synthetic brain juice," Harrumphrey explained.

"Yick." Elliot flicked it back into the tub.

"Actually, it's quite ingenious," said his uncle. He joined them on the edge of the wooden patio. "As you know, we weren't having the best of luck with the cerebellows, so we decided to try something new." He spread his arm over the water. "And what's a better way to stimulate creativity than splashing around in a hot, bubbling bath of brain fluid?"

"Have you tried Sudoku?" asked Leslie, frowning at the orange foam.

"Don't knock it 'til you try it," said Patti Mudmeyer, the bog nymph. She had popped out of the water, resting her scaly elbows on the edge of the deck. "It's like *breathing* creativity!"

"I wouldn't know," Harrumphrey grumbled. "I don't have gills."

"Too bad for you," said Patti, smiling brightly as orange fluid leaked from the slits on either side of her neck.

"What about you two?" asked the professor, turning to Elliot and Leslie. "Care for a dip?"

Leslie shook her head. "*Us?* In a tub of brain juice?!"

The professor nodded. "It might help with those clever anti-ghork devices you've been working on."

Elliot's uncle had a point. Ever since their last adventure, Elliot and Leslie had been spending all their free time at DENKi-3000. The professor had charged them with the task of designing a series of devices that could be used against the ghorks, in the event of another attack.

"I don't think that's necessary," said Elliot. He was quite confident in the devices he and Leslie had designed. He pointed to the bizarre blueprints, pinned to a corkboard against the wall. "I think they're perfect!"

"Maybe you do," said the professor, "but let's not forget: Sometimes, our inventions don't work precisely the way we plan."

"You got that right, Doc," said Patti. "Remember my invisibility machine?"

"You mean *almost*-invisibility machine," Harrumphrey corrected.

"Exactly. That *definitely* didn't work according to plan."

"All it did was make things blurry," said Elliot.

"You got it, kiddo. And now that Sir William has promoted Charlton the cycloptosaurus to head of marketing, my poor old invention has been shrunk down and rebranded as The Impressionisticator™. They tell me it's s'posed to appeal to *interior decorators*, ones who wanna make a room look like a hazy oil painting from nineteenth-century Paris." She shrugged. "Definitely a niche market."

"You think zat is bad?" asked Jean-Remy. "Have you seen how zey are using my beautiful Tele-Pathetic Helmet? Zey are using the technology in cinemas! Now whenever zey show ze audience a sappy movie zey can make sure ze people cry at just ze right time."

Gügor thumped forward, a glum expression on his already glum face. "That's nothing," he said. "It was *Gügor's* invention that was turned into the silliest one!" The knucklecrumpler pointed a thick orange finger toward the Rickem-Ruckery Room.

Standing beside the entrance was a refrigerator shaped like a snowman, with three round doors, one on top of another, with a a goofy grin and a plastic carrot-nose stuck to the top. "Because Gügor's teleportation device sent everything to the South Pole, the marketing people turned it into The Frosti-Friend™. When you open his belly, you can chill frozen peas in an ice cave in Antarctica."

"Actually," said Leslie, "that sounds like a pretty good idea. If Grandpa Freddy was here, I'll bet he'd like to have one of those in his kitchen."

"It does have a certain appeal," admitted the professor. "In fact, Sir William has taken Charlton on a month-long tour to promote the company's new products at technology exhibitions around the world."

"Hold on a second," said Elliot. "What about rocket boots? The marketing department *couldn't* have rebranded those, right? I mean . . . they're rocket boots! Everybody and their pet duck wants a pair of rocket boots!"

Leslie rolled her eyes. "Why would *a duck* want rocket boots? They have wings."

"It's a figure of speech."

"I think you mean everybody and their *dog*."

Elliot shrugged. "I like to do my own thing."

Leslie's eyes moved down to Elliot's bright green fishing vest. "Have you ever thought of doing *someone else's* thing—just for once?"

Elliot narrowed his eyes. "Why are you staring at my vest?"

"Have you ever considered not wearing it *every* day?"

Elliot folded his arms tightly across his chest, almost as if to challenge anyone to *even try* to take off his most prized piece of clothing. "I thought we were talking about rocket boots," he said defiantly.

Leslie rolled her eyes again. All she could think of to say was "*Ugh!*"

"Indeed," said Elliot's uncle. "Rocket boots. I'm certain they'll be a huge hit, just as soon as they're approved by the Federal Aviation Authority. Unfortunately, that could take *years*."

"Patience," said Gügor. "There's an old saying in Gügor's family. It goes like this: *Crumple, crumple, crumple, crumple, crumple . . .*" He went on like this for quite a while, counting off "crumples" one by one on his enormous fingers. ". . . *crumple, crumple, crumple, crumple*—come to think of it, maybe there isn't enough time to finish this saying." He scratched his head. "It has something to do with patience."

"Yes," said the professor. "Patience. Very important! In the meantime, however, we'll need some new ideas. Let's see what we've come up with." He pointed a remote control into the shadows of the ceiling. With the press of a button, a view-screen descended out of the darkness. On it was a list of strange inventions:

Shoehorn Horn

Karate Chop Sticks

Creature Reacher

Ty-Spoon

Fright Bulb

Igloo Glue

Un-Brella

Tentacle Extender

Flying Pan

"What's a 'shoehorn horn'?" asked Leslie.

"Isn't it obvious?" harrumphed Harrumphrey.

"Probably only to the person who invented it. Wait. That was you, wasn't it?"

Harrumphrey nodded proudly.

"Well, to me it just sounds kooky."

Harrumphrey put on the glowering expression for which he was renowned.

"You do know," he said, "what a regular shoehorn is. Right?"

Leslie nodded. "One of those little plastic tongue-thingies, for slipping your heel into a shoe."

"Exactly. That's a shoehorn. A shoehorn *horn* is a regular shoehorn with a little trumpet at the top."

"Why does it need a little trumpet?" asked Elliot.

"*Duh!* So you know when your shoe's on. The moment your heel touches down, the shoehorn horn plays 'When the Saints Go Marching In'!"

Leslie folded her arms. "Do people really need an alarm to tell them their shoes are on?"

Harrumphrey nodded gravely. "I'm still working on the practical applications."

"How about a Fright Bulb?" asked Elliot. "That sounds interesting."

"It's one of mine," said Patti.

The bog nymph pulled herself out of the Think Tank and onto the deck. "You know how everyone's kinda scared of the dark?"

"Not me," said Leslie. She spun side to side to show off her black tights, black dress, and black T-shirt. "For me, dark is the new pink."

"Trust me, hon, you're in the minority there." Patti wrung

out her kelp-like hair. Rivulets of her clay-colored scalp resin ran down her scaly back. "Most people hate the dark. They're afraid of it. Hard to believe, I know. But that's where the Fright Bulb comes in." She leaned over the edge of the deck. "Show 'em the prototype, Gügor."

From a nearby cabinet, Gügor took a small wooden box with a lightbulb screwed into it. On the bulb's glass was a stylized drawing of a face with ghostly features, angry eyes, and a snarling mouth. When Gügor flicked the switch on the box, the bulb blossomed an eerie phosphorescent green, and the face said:

"*Boo!*"

"Y'see?" said Patti. "The Fright Bulb is the opposite of a regular *light*bulb. It scares you when you turn *on* the lights."

"That one might need some work, too," said Leslie.

Patti sucked her teeth. "Another niche market, right?"

"I'd say so."

Elliot sighed. "Are any of these actually *good* ideas?"

"*Mais, bien sûr!* You have not yet talked about *my idea*!" Jean-Remy flew forward to hover halfway between the viewscreen and the orange bubbles of the Think Tank. He pointed to the last invention on the list. "Ze Flying Pan!"

"Do you mean *frying* pan?" asked Leslie. "I hate to tell you, but those have already been invented."

"*No-no-no!* Not ze frying pan, ze *flying* pan. It is just like ze regular pan, only with ze flapping wings! Like mine." Jean-Remy demonstrated by fluttering in an elegant loop.

Elliot rolled his eyes. "Wings on a frying pan? That makes even less sense than putting rocket boots on a duck."

Jean-Remy covered his heart as if he had been wounded. "Oh! How can you say such a thing?!"

Leslie shrugged. "You have to admit, it's hard to see the sense in a flying pan."

"Let me explain. You know ze times when you flip ze *crêpe* in ze pan, but you flip it too high or too much to one side? What can you do? Do you run after ze beautiful *crêpe*, carrying ze hot pan? No-no-no! *C'est trop dangereux!* But *zees* pan—zees beautiful *flying* pan—it can glide through ze air, as graceful as . . . as . . . as ze *fairy-bat*! It catches ze *crêpe*—perfectly flat—*every time!*" Having concluded, Jean-Remy tipped in the air to fall into a low bow.

Leslie looked at Elliot. "Actually, that sounds almost . . . *useful.*"

"We do have a flying pan prototype in development," said the professor, "but let's face it—it's yet another product with only a niche market. What we need is something more universal, something that would appeal to everyone, to the whole wo—"

DING-A-LING-A-LING-A-LINNNNNG!

The conversation was interrupted by the sound of an old bell. It was followed by a pair of shrill voices, crying out in unison.

"Mail call!"

Elliot and Leslie looked down from the deck. They saw Bildorf and Pib, the two rat-like hobmongrels. They were both wearing blue caps with shiny black visors, the sort of uniforms worn by postal workers. Pib, the taller (and mangier) of the two, was pushing a huge cart loaded with envelopes and packages, while her companion, Bildorf, marched out in front of it. In his hand he carried a golden bell, which he shook again for added emphasis.

DING-A-LING-A-LING-A-LINNNNG!

"Mail call!"

Harrumphrey groaned. "Whose bright idea was it to give them *a bell*?"

"Quit gripin'," said Patti. "Just be glad they decided to take on some responsibility for once."

"It's Reggie we have to thank," said the professor. "Ever since those two befriended him, they've given up devoting their lives to mischief and wisecracks. Thank goodness!"

"We'll see how long it lasts," Harrumphrey harrumphed.

Bildorf and Pib pushed the mail cart around the laboratory, delivering postcards, envelopes, and packages to delighted creatures of all shapes and sizes.

They handed Jean-Remy a delicate envelope. The moment he saw it, his face went even paler than usual. He flew up to perch on the edge of the Think Tank, staring at the envelope.

"Whatcha got there, JR?" asked Patti.

Jean-Remy didn't answer. He opened the envelope and tugged out a single page. The moment he began to unfold it, there was a swell of music, the mournful whine of a hundred violins. He slapped the paper shut. The music stopped.

"What was *that*?" asked Elliot.

"Sounds to me like a singing telegram," said Harrumphrey, "and judging by the tone of those violins, it's not good news."

Jean-Remy slid the folded page gently between his fingers. "It's from my sister," he said. He opened the letter all the way, and the same keening music filled the laboratory.

Then the telegram began to sing. . . .

CHAPTER 2

In which Reggie's paunch packs a punch

eep in the tunnels below the Creature Department, Colonel-Admiral Reginald T. Pusslegut was listening. He was quite adept at hearing things. He was a regimental bombastadon, after all, native to the vast white wastes of Antarctica. When you were swatting away berg-biters in the midst of a blizzard, you certainly couldn't rely on your *eyes* to save you.

There were no berg-biters here, however. What Reggie heard was something else, but something just as unsettling.

Footsteps!

This came as a surprise. Over the past few weeks, the tunnels below the Creature Department had fallen eerily quiet. Prior to the great melee the creatures now called the Battle of Bickleburgh, Reggie could expect at least a *weekly* scuffle with the odd ghork. But he hadn't drawn his ceremonial saber in ages! Now, however, he placed one hand on the hilt.

They were coming closer. Clomping, clumping, lumbering footsteps. This wasn't the sound from *just one* pair of feet. No, this sounded more like . . .

Three.

Or four.

Or six!

"Oh, dear," Reggie whispered to himself.

That was when they emerged from the darkness around the corner. Not three, not four, not even six, but *seven nose-ghorks!* They pumped their arms and raised their knees high with every step, thumping their feet so hard their ample reserves of snot were shaken loose. With every second step, a long pendulum of mucus swung a little lower.

SLOOORP!

All seven ghorks snorted in unison, and each string of slime was vacuumed up into their tremendous schnozzes.

"*Halt!*" Reggie drew his ceremonial saber (at last) and brandished it at the group. "Identify yourselves!"

"What's the matter?" said the leader. "You've never heard of Whiffer and the Sniffle-Snufflers?"

"It is my great pleasure to inform you that I have not."

The nose-ghork who called himself Whiffer seemed shocked. "You're kidding! We're famous."

"Your entirely self-proclaimed renown," boomed Reggie, "is no concern of mine. Your *destination*, however, is of the utmost consequence!" To demonstrate his seriousness, he puffed out his chest and raised his ceremonial saber even higher. "I cannot let you pass."

Whiffer, seeing he outnumbered Reggie seven-to-one, was unfazed by this warning. His beady eyes scanned up and down the bombastadon's bulky body. "Like I'm gonna take orders from a blubbery butterball dressed up like a shopping mall security guard."

Reggie's jowls trembled with indignation. "*Security guard?!* Outrageous! This is the very uniform I wore while bringing peace to the vast wilds of—"

Whiffer snapped his fingers. "Would somebody please *pop* this air bag?"

The six other ghorks leapt at Reggie. Three of them latched onto his arm, rattling his ceremonial saber until it clanged to the cold stone floor.

"*Scoundrels!* You might've cracked its immaculate golden finish!"

"We'll crack a lot more than that," snorted one of the ghorks.

All seven of them strained to push Reggie against the wall. He indeed cracked the back of his head against it—though the sound was less of a *crack* and more of a *splodge*. That was because Reggie's skull was covered with just as much blubber as the rest of him. Instead of being knocked unconscious, he was merely dazed. He slumped to the floor, where the ghorks piled on top of him, pinning him down. At last, Whiffer leapt right on top of Reggie's belly.

"*Oof!*"

The lead ghork leaned forward and flared his bottomless nostrils. Two strings of snot dangled above Reggie's face, ready to drop at the merest sniffle.

"Get away from me, you putrid, mucilaginous scamp!" Reggie tried to wrestle free, but it was no use. "You can not, and will not, pass!"

Whiffer sloorped the twin boogers back up his nose. He peered down the tunnel where Reggie was looking. It was the one that led to DENKi-3000 Headquarters. "Down there? Who ever said we wanted to go down there?"

Reggie was confused. "You mean you're not here to besiege the Creature Department, to imprison my friends, and steal our wondrous inventions?"

Whiffer snorted. "Besieging is *so* last week." He stooped even closer to Reggie's face. "This time we've got a much better plan."

"And what might that be?"

Whiffer chuckled. "Like I'm gonna tell you."

Oh, but you must, thought Reggie. *It is imperative!* As the Creature Department's honorary part-time security guard, it was his solemn duty to extract information. But in his current position, he couldn't do it with force. No, this called for . . . what was the word? (Reggie had never paid much attention to the subtler forms of combat, back at the Antarctic military academy. He was a bombastadon, after all. They were hardly known for subtlety.) What *was* it again? *Diverse* psychology? No, that wasn't it. *Perverse* psychology? Definitely not! Oh, yes, now he remembered. . . .

"*Ooooooh!*" he said to Whiffer, rolling his squinty bombastadon eyes. "Now I get it. You *don't have* any plan at all. Well! I should have known. Ghorks never do!"

Whiffer stomped one foot into Reggie's gut.

"*Oof!*"

"Yes, we do! Our plans are the best! Right, guys?"

The other ghorks produced nasally murmurs of agreement.

Reggie shook his head in feigned disappointment. "Is that so? And when was the last time a ghork plan worked? Tell me that."

Whiffer looked to his friends. "Remember that time we planned a surprise retirement party for old Nostrildamus?"

The other ghorks laughed.

"That was some bash!" said one of them.

"He never saw it coming!" cried another.

Reggie smiled. "A surprise retirement party? That's the finest thing you've ever planned? Pitiful! I believe you've just proved my point—you ghorks can't plan *anything*!"

Whiffer gritted his teeth. He leaned close to Reggie's face. "Not this time," he whispered. "See, this time we're not going to boring old Bickleburgh." He pointed into the darkness of the other tunnel. "We're going down there, to Simmersville. It's all been planned. That's where we're gonna have the Great Hexposé!"

Reggie was pleased at having loosened Whiffer's tongue, but he had no idea what the ghork was talking about. "I beg your pardon," he said. "The great *what*?"

Whiffer's eyes clouded with a misty brand of madness. "The Great Hexposé!"

Reggie raised his head off the floor. "Look here! I would appreciate a straight answer, you loony! You can't simply repeat the name of the mysterious event in a dreamy voice and expect me to understand! In any case, I'm quite certain you're mispronouncing the word. I believe what you mean to say is *exposé*."

"No, I mean *Hex*posé." Whiffer straightened himself, still atop the plump summit of Reggie's belly, and tapped his temple. "We ghorks, we're smarter than we look, see?"

"*Smart?*" said Reggie. "You, sir, look about as intellectually adept as a warm stream of your own snot-rocketry!"

Whiffer stomped his other foot.

"*Oof!*"

"Hex has two meanings," said Whiffer, puffing out his narrow chest. "First, it means the number six, get it? And second . . ." He held up two fingers. "It means *a curse*. It's the curse of an ancient Ghorkolian prophecy. The prophecy of *the Sixth Ghork*!"

Reggie now found himself in what was (for him) an unusual

situation. He didn't know what to say. How could there possibly be a Sixth Ghork? In all of creaturedom, there were only *five kinds* of the despicable villains. Nose-ghorks, like these ones pinning him to the floor, along with the mouth-ghorks, eye-ghorks, ear-ghorks, and hand-ghorks. One, two, three, four, five . . . but a sixth? *Preposterous!*

"The prophecy says that when we find him, we'll be unstoppable!" Whiffer leaned even closer to Reggie's face. "And guess what, blubber-butt? Grinner and the others *have found him*! They're going to unveil him at the Great Hexposé and that's only the beginning."

The beginning of what? thought Reggie.

"Of course," said Whiffer, "now that we've told you, we have to make sure you don't tell anyone else." The ghork sniffled, and two pillars of snot slithered toward Reggie's face like a pair of glistening green pythons. Reggie yanked on his arms and legs, but the ghorks pinning him down wouldn't budge. For a regimental bombastadon, however, arms and legs played only a small role in hand-to-hand combat. In fact, at that very moment, Whiffer was crouched on top of Reggie's greatest weapon.

His belly.

It had been a long time since Reggie had performed a Bombastadon Belly Bounce Maneuver. It was potentially quite a dangerous (not to mention mathematically challenging) defensive technique, and ought to be employed only in the most desperate of situations. This was surely one of them, wasn't it?

He took a deep breath, casting his eyes over the cave's geography. Without a blackboard and an abacus, he couldn't be certain the math was correct, but he would have to chance it.

"What's the matter?" Whiffer sneered. "You scared? That why your face is all red? Don't worry. It'll all be over in—"

BA-BOOM!

Reggie exhaled and flexed his monumental belly muscles. Instantly, Whiffer bounded off Reggie's paunch and somersaulted up to the ceiling of the cave. When he came back down, Reggie angled his belly to bounce him straight into two of his compatriots. The trio flew off in three different directions, ricocheted off the walls, and returned to hit the remaining four. Soon, all seven ghorks were flailing across the room, bounding off Reggie's belly as if it were a fiendish trampoline.

At last, Reggie altered the angle and sent all seven ghorks thumping into the wall, where they slumped down into a bruised and dizzy heap. Then Colonel-Admiral Reginald T. Pusslegut climbed to his feet and retrieved his ceremonial saber from where it had (unceremoniously) fallen. He hoisted up Whiffer by the scruff of his neck and pointed his saber into the ghork's face. "I want you to tell me everything you know about this so-called Sixth Ghork."

"I'm not . . . telling you . . . squat," Whiffer panted. "And guess what, you're not the only one with fancy moves. Watch this!"

SLOOOOOOOOORRRP!

All seven ghorks discharged the full contents of their prolific sinuses at Reggie. In an instant, his beautiful uniform was ruined, and he was soaked to his blubbery skin with a gooey, gluey (and disgustingly warm) muck. Taking advantage of Reggie's sliminess, Whiffer slipped free of the bombastadon's grip. He and the rest of his gang scampered into the shadows of the tunnel toward Simmersville.

Reggie's first thought was to chase them, but with only a single step, he slipped head over heels into a slimy puddle of his own drippings.

"Mucilaginous scamps," he muttered.

CHAPTER 3

In which Jean-Remy surprises everyone,
and Gügor surprises Jean-Remy

t the top of Jean-Remy's telegram, a jungle of curlicues
and flourishes surrounded these words:

Wail Mail Inc.

~ When you need your message to get through LOUD and CLEAR! ~

(Delivering fine musical Yell-A-Grams to all of creaturedom, since 1602)

"Look," said Leslie, pointing to the page. "Something
happened to the letter!"

A third of the way down the page, a jagged gash cut across
the words. The letter appeared to be torn almost completely
in two.

"Don't worry," said Harrumphrey. "That's not a tear. It's
a mouth."

"A mouth?" asked Elliot.

"Of course," said Patti. "It's a singing telegram."

Jean-Remy opened the page a little farther and it suddenly

came to life, fluttering in his hands. The tear creased itself into a distinct pair of lips, and the telegram began to sing:

My dearest BROTHER!

Something TERRIBLE has happened! I know it's been a long time, but please believe me; I had NO CHOICE but to write! Because I NEED YOUR HELP! After you left Paris all those years ago, I missed you TERRIBLY, and so I followed you across an OCEAN! I've tried to find you so many times!

I thought I had LOST YOU, lost track of you completely, but then I saw the news of the BRAVE BATTLE you and your friends fought against those insufferable ghorks! What a surprise to discover all this time you've been working in a creature depart-ment not far from my own! The company where I work is called HEPPLEWORTH'S HEALTH FOOD! At our factory we make the most delicious dishes you can possibly imagine!

Or at least we USED TO!

(Here, the violins spiraled down through a cascade of minor notes.)

OH! Oh-oh-oh-oh-OOOOOH! Oh! Oh, yes, my dear Jean-Remy, YOU MUST HELP US! Quazicom and the ghorks have taken over the HEPPLEWORTH FOOD FACTORY! This very weekend, at our city's ANNUAL FOOOOOD FESTIVAAAAAAAL, they are planning something

TRUUUULY HORRENDOOOOUS!

YOU and your FRIENDS are our only hope! I know we've had our differences in the past, but please, brother . . . WILL YOU HEEELLP UUUUUUUSSS?!

Your sister!

Eloise-Yvette!

The song ended with the five dainty syllables of *El-o-ise-Y-vette*, tinkling off what sounded like a xylophone. On the final *plink*, everyone applauded. (It was the respectable thing to do. The telegram had an exceptional voice.)

"You have a *sister*?" asked Harrumphrey. He was as surprised as everyone else.

Jean-Remy nodded. "Eloise-Yvette. Zat was her voice. But zis telegram? No, it can only be a fake."

"You callin' me a liar?" asked the telegram. Its voice was no longer that of an angelic soprano. Now it sounded more like a New York cabbie. "Listen, buddy, this here's the genuine article. I was there when your sis wrote it!"

Jean-Remy crumpled the paper.

"*Hey!* Watch where you're foldin' that, buddy!"

Jean-Remy flew across the laboratory and dropped the telegram in the trash bin.

Elliot couldn't believe it. "Jean-Remy! What's the matter with you? What if it's not a fake?"

"It must be," said Jean-Remy. "*Ma soeur?* She does not work in some nearby *food factory*! She is in Paris! Probably singing in some seedy club under ze street!"

"What if she's not?" asked Elliot. "She said she followed you here."

Jean-Remy stubbornly refused to believe the telegram was genuine. "No," he said, slicing his hand through the air as if to cut off further discussion. "It is not true."

"Oh, yes it is," said Leslie, "and I can prove it."

Jean-Remy paused, hovering in the air.

"You can?" Elliot looked at his friend. "How?"

"The food festival," Leslie explained. "The Simmersville Food Festival. Heppleworth's Health Food is the main sponsor. I know all about it because every year there's a big market square where chefs come from all over to set up stalls and show off their new dishes. Grandpa Freddy goes every year, and I was hoping he'd be back in time, but . . . well, it doesn't seem like he's gonna make it." Leslie hung her head. "This year it'll just be me and my mom."

"Okay," said Elliot, "but what does that have to do with the telegram? I thought you said you could prove—"

"*I can*. Jean-Remy's sister mentioned the food festival. It's famous, but not *that* famous. How would she know about it if she lived in Paris? She must be working at Heppleworth's!"

Jean-Remy floated down to Leslie. "Zat does not prove anything. Anyone could have penned ze telegram."

Elliot was still confused. "Why don't you want to help your sister?"

Jean-Remy sighed. "You do not understand. Even if ze telegram is real—which it is not—why would I want to help a sister like Eloise-Yvette? She is vain and selfish and cannot be trusted!"

Everyone was shocked to hear this. How could Jean-Remy, so beloved by everyone, have someone like that for a sister?

"*No*," said a slow, deep voice, from over near the trash bin where Jean-Remy had just discarded the singing telegram. "Eloise-Yvette isn't like that at all."

It was Gügor. He had reached into the bin with his enormous knucklecrumpler hand and fished out the envelope.

Jean-Remy narrowed his eyes, regarding the knucklecrumpler suspiciously. "And how," he asked, "would you know?"

Gügor looked down at the floor and, to everyone's surprise, *he blushed*. "Because . . ." he said at last, "Eloise-Yvette is Gügor's 1TL."

Jean-Remy narrowed his eyes. "1TL? What does zees mean, *1TL?*"

Gügor took a deep breath. "One. True. Love."

For the second time that morning, the laboratory fell silent. Jean-Remy zipped across the room and stopped so abruptly in front of Gügor's face, you could almost make out the skid marks he left floating in the air behind him.

"My sister? Eloise-Yvette? *Your one true love?!*"

Gügor nodded sheepishly.

"You had better explain yourself, my friend."

"Okay. But if you want to know Gügor's story, I'll have to start at the beginning. . . ."

CHAPTER 4

In which Gügor tells his tale

ügor wasn't kidding—his story really did begin at the
beginning.

"Gügor was born the youngest in his family," he
explained. "Gügor had thirty-six brothers and sisters!"

Patti whistled sympathetically. "*Thirty-six?!* I've only got
the three myself. Sisters, that is—and I can hardly stand 'em!"

Gügor explained his early days, growing up on Mount
Squash, the ancestral home of knucklecrumplers. "Gügor's parents wanted him to follow in the family footsteps, and get a job
crumpling things with his hands. But Gügor wanted to know
why. 'Because it's tradition,' said Gügor's father. 'And look at
these hands, son. It's what knucklecrumplers are *made for.*'"
Gügor held up his own hands, showing off his big knucklecrumpler mitts to everyone in the laboratory.

"He had a point," said Elliot. "Your dad, I mean."

Gügor nodded. "Yes, but Gügor didn't want to crumple
things just for the sake of crumpling things. Gügor wanted to
make things . . . by crumpling things. That's rickem-ruckery,
fixing machines—or even inventing new ones—with nothing but

your bare hands." Gügor smiled a goofy grin and poked one big thumb into his chest. "Gügor has an advanced degree in applied rickem-ruckery from Mount Squash College! After graduation, Gügor went off to make his fortune! That was how Gügor ended up in Paris, where he met Eloise-Yvette."

"Why Paris?" asked Leslie. She was curious, and besides, it was a city she had always dreamed of visiting.

"Yes," said Jean-Remy, "why Paris—and where does my sister come into all of zis?!"

Gügor lowered his voice. "Not everyone knows this, but lots of creatures live in the catacombs underneath the city. Four-eyed snoods and triple-bearded oven trolls, even a few marrowwranglers, who are distant cousins of us knucklecrumplers. Gügor met them all. Most of them were artists and writers and musicians, of course. Except in Paris they had a special word for them."

"*Unemployed*," said Harrumphrey.

"No," said Gügor. "Bohemians. When Gügor showed them his rickem-ruckery skills, they gave him a job inventing instruments to play in their underground jazz clubs. Gügor was so proud! His first real job! Gügor even learned to play one of his very own creations: a steam-powered electrombone!"

"You play electrombone?" asked the professor. He seemed quite impressed.

Gügor nodded proudly. "Gügor *invented* the electrombone!"

"Smarter than he looks," Harrumphrey quipped.

"Eventually, Gügor began performing with the other creatures." He chewed his lip and glanced at Jean-Remy. "That was how I met Eloise-Yvette. They had a special name for her, too. She was called the Bluebird."

Jean-Remy nodded. "I remember. It was her stage name, on

account of her sapphire skin and what I can *only assume* was her melancholy singing voice. I never went to see her perform. I wanted nothing do to with her ridiculous '*Bohemian*' friends."

Gügor sighed. "If you had come, you would have seen Gügor perform, too. On his electrombone! They called us 'The Bluebird and the Brute.'" Gügor hung his head. "I'm sure you can guess who 'the Brute' was."

Leslie patted the back of Gügor's big warm hand. "We know you're not really a brute. At least not when you're in the Rickem-Ruckery Room."

"Thank you. But next to Eloise-Yvette, that was how Gügor felt." The knucklecrumpler's shoulders fell, and he sighed heavily. "She probably thought the same thing. That was why Gügor never told her how he felt. Gügor never told *anybody* how he felt. Not even you, Jean-Remy . . . until today."

"Aw, Gügor, you poor thing! I know just how you feel. Maybe a bit like this." Patti ran one hand through her seaweed hair. She came out with a lump of silt and sculpted it into a tiny heart, complete with a jagged crack down the middle. She held it up for him to see.

Gügor nodded.

"But if you don't tell her how you feel," Patti went on, "then you'll never have a chance to do this." She gently squeezed the heart, and the crack vanished.

Gügor shook his head. He twisted his toes nervously into the laboratory floor. "Gügor is shy."

"Everybody's shy sometimes," said Leslie. "My mom used to move us around so much, I was always new in town. I hated going up and introducing myself to the other kids, but sometimes that's what you have to do. You just have to tell people how you feel."

"So that's what we're gonna do," said Elliot. "We're going to Simmersville, we're going to rescue Jean-Remy's sister, and Gügor is going to tell her how he really—"

"*No, no, no!*" Jean-Remy swooped down between Elliot and the others. "I told you. Ze telegram is a fake!"

Gügor opened the letter and sniffed it. "It smells like Eloise-Yvette. She always wore Lait de la Lune perfume."

Jean-Remy sighed. "Okay, let us say—*hypozetically*—the telegram is real, and zis city, Simmersville, it has been infiltrated with ghorks, and yes, my sister and her friends, zey have been kidnapped. Perhaps it is all true—which I do not believe it is—but *if* it is, yes, we must go and rescue her. But Gügor! My friend! Do you really crave ze love of someone like *my sister*? Someone so vain and selfish, who cannot be trusted?"

Gügor frowned. "That doesn't sound like Eloise-Yvette at all."

Leslie and Elliot couldn't understand the discrepancy between Gügor and Jean-Remy's versions of Eloise-Yvette. How could they be talking about the same fairy-bat?

"I don't get it," said Leslie. "What's up with you and your sister?"

Jean-Remy sighed. "I don't like to talk about it," he said. And that was all.

"Maybe if you did, we'd be able to under—"

Leslie was interrupted when the doors at the far end of the laboratory slammed open and a big blubbery figure came slopping across the floor. It was Reggie. He was dripping with something slimy. With every *plonk* of his enormous galoshes, the huge bombastadon dribbled a trail of what could only be described as . . . *snot*.

"What happened to you?" asked the professor.

"*Ghorks*," Reggie muttered. "With insidiously exaggerated nasal passages."

Harrumphrey sighed. "Not again. We just finished cleaning up after the last time!"

"Fear not, my friends," said Reggie. He shivered his epaulettes and spattered several laboratory tables with mucus. Two globs sailed clear across the room and hit Bildorf and Pib.

"Hey! You did that on purpose," cried Pib, "and you've completely *ruined* our uniforms!"

"*Yick*," said Bildorf, doffing his postman's cap. "You can expect a hefty dry cleaning bill, you big blubbery bonehead!"

"As I was saying," Reggie continued, ignoring the complaints of the hobmongrels, "I don't believe we have anything to fear . . . at least for the time being. No attack on the Creature Department is imminent. In fact, the ghorks don't appear to be interested in DENKi-3000 at all."

"That's a new one," said Harrumphrey.

"Yes, quite." Reggie poked his lower lip out thoughtfully between his tusks. "Apparently, they are preparing to fulfill some sort of ancient Ghorkolian prophecy."

"That doesn't sound good," said Patti.

"What sort of prophecy?" asked the professor.

Reggie explained what he had discovered about the so-called "Great Hexposé" of the Fabled Sixth Ghork.

"A *sixth* ghork? How could there be a . . ." The professor trailed off, obviously unsure of what to make of this news. He looked around at his creaturely colleagues. "Has anyone ever heard of a sixth ghork?"

They all shook their heads. Elliot and Leslie were just as dumbfounded. They looked at each other, wondering the very same thing: *What would a sixth ghork be like?*

"No way," said Patti. "That's nothing but pure, down-home *hooey*! There's only five kinds of them bozos. Ever'body knows that!"

"That's what we all *assume*." Reggie puffed out his floppy jowls. "But what if it's not quite accurate? What if this Fabled Sixth Ghork truly does exist? What could it mean?"

"A ghork with a sixth sense," Elliot whispered.

"With psychic powers," said Leslie.

"Like telepathy."

"Telekinesis."

"Predicting the future."

"A ghork with that kind of power," said Harrumphrey, "could mean the end of creaturedom as we know it."

The professor looked to Reggie. "Did you find out anything else?"

The bombastadon stroked his flabby chin. "Not a great deal. Merely that the insufferable cretin was headed to join the rest of his monstrous friends in some nearby hamlet. He called it . . . Simmersville, I believe."

Leslie's eyes popped wide. "So it *is* true. The ghorks really are in Simmersville. I knew it!"

"Sounds to me like it's time to save the day," said the professor, unable to suppress the note of hopeful excitement in his voice. "The only question left is: *How best to get there?*"

CHAPTER 5

In which Leslie suggests disguises (that aren't disguises),
Harrumphrey explains the skepticism of computers,
and Reggie zaps himself

ow to get there?" asked Patti. "That's the least of our troubles! You expect us to just waltz into town without anyone noticing? Look at us. In case you've forgotten— *we're a bunch of creatures*!"

Patti had a point. For generations, the DENKi-3000 Creature Department had remained a closely guarded secret, the inner workings of the company hidden from the citizens of Bickleburgh. Following the attack of the ghorks, some of the locals were (perhaps, somewhat) accustomed to the idea of having creatures for neighbors, but they nevertheless preferred them to remain out of sight.

Simmersville was two or three hours away by car. It was safe to assume all the same rules applied there. If the Heppleworth Food Factory had its own Creature Department, it would also be a secret. In fact, it was unlikely anyone in Simmersville knew anything about the strange, hidden world of creaturedom.

"I'm sure half of Simmersville would faint dead right away if we suddenly went capering up the main street of town." The professor looked around the laboratory at his department of creaturely inventors. "I doubt they've seen anything as outlandish as you guys before!"

"Oh, yes they have!" said Leslie. "And that's exactly how we can sneak into town undetected."

"Do you mean to imply," Reggie inquired, "the people of Simmersville are *familiar* with the creatures of creaturedom?"

Leslie shook her head. "Not creatures, no. But what they *do* know is . . . *costumed cabaret!*"

The professor furrowed his brow. "I'm not sure I follow."

"The timing couldn't be more perfect," Leslie explained. "Every year, the Simmersville Food Festival ends with a big dinner-theatre-style cabaret, right in the main square. It's super-cool!"

"*Cool?*" Elliot couldn't believe what he was hearing. "How is it possible you think my fishing vest is dorky, but you like *dinner-theatre-style cabaret?*"

"It's possible," Leslie answered, "because your fishing vest *is* dorky."

"It is not!" Elliot waved his hands up and down the vest. "Look at how many pockets I've got!"

"I think you just proved my point," said Leslie.

"There is *no way* a cabaret is cooler than my fishing vest! You only have to say it. Dinner-theatre-style costume cabaret! It sounds like the sort of show old people go to see in Las Vegas."

Leslie shut her eyes. "Have you ever been to Las Vegas?"

"No," Elliot grumbled.

"And have you ever been to a dinner-theatre-style costume cabaret?"

Elliot hesitated. "Well . . . no," he said at last.

"Then let me finish explaining." Leslie moved her eyes over the creatures, who by now were curiously crowding around her. "Trust me, guys. No matter how weird you think *you* look, you'll have no problems in Simmersville—at least not this weekend. It's all because of the cabaret. The performers dress up in the weirdest, most outrageous costumes you can think of. All we have to do is tell people that's what you are—*cabaret performers*—and you'll fit right in."

"Is that true?" asked Gügor. He spread his arms and thumped around in a circle. "Even as weird as Gügor?"

"*Weirder*," said Leslie. She tugged on the bottom of her T-shirt, pulling the fabric out to show everyone the silk-screen print. "As weird as *this*."

Leslie's T-shirt was emblazoned with a stage photograph of her favorite band, Boris Minor and the Karloffs. They were famous for performing in costumes that looked like monsters from old black-and-white horror movies. Everyone leaned in for a closer look. When they saw the band, the creatures nodded to one another. Leslie was right; they certainly didn't look any stranger than Boris Minor and the Karloffs.

Leslie's face lit up as she pointed to the picture. "And *guess* who's playing the big finale in the cabaret this year!"

"*Them?*" asked Elliot. He had only heard a few of their songs (the ones Leslie had *forced* him to listen to), and he was fairly certain the two of them would never see eye-to-eye when it came to music. "Didn't they split up? Like, *before we were even born?*"

Leslie shrugged. "They get back together for special events, like the Simmersville Food Festival Dinner-Theatre-Style Costume Cabaret."

"Oh, brother," said Elliot.

"Leslie might be on to something," said the professor. "But if we're going to pass as cabaret performers, we'll definitely have to practice some dance moves." He made two fists, tucked his elbows into his ribs, and shimmied his hips.

Patti winced at the professor's one-man samba (crossed with "The Chicken Dance"). "Some of us," she groaned, "are gonna need *a teensy bit* more practice than others."

Harrumphrey stomped his foot. "*Some of us* aren't going to practice at all. Because *some of us* don't dance. Don't sing, either. And *definitely* don't do cabaret!"

"I get the feeling yer referrin' to yourself there," said Patti.

Harrumphrey nodded his enormous cranium. "*Huffleheads don't dance.*"

"A hufflehead? Is that what you are? I always took you for a glowerpuss."

Harrumphrey ignored Patti's comment. "While I admit Leslie's idea does possess a modicum of validity, there is *no way in all of creaturedom* you'll get me doing a song-and-dance number."

"Don't knock it till you try it," said Patti.

In response, Harrumphrey did what he did best. He harrumphed.

"I think it's a *capital* idea!" said Reggie. He puffed out his chest (even more than usual). "Back in my regimental days I had *quite* the reputation as a submaritone."

"A what?" asked Elliot. "There's no such thing." He lifted his fingers and counted off the male voice types he remembered from music class. "Tenor, baritone, bass, basso profundo, and . . . well, that's it. There's nothing after basso profundo."

"Of course there is, my boy!" Reggie lifted his brow

indignantly (you could just about make out his eyes under the bulge of forehead blubber). "*Submaritone!* 'Deep as a submarine,' as they say. Look here, I'll give you a demonstration." Reggie sucked in a deep breath and—

"Not now, Reggie," said the professor. "We'll practice later. First, we have planning to do. If the ghorks have taken control of the Heppleworth Food Factory, they'll be on the lookout for intruders. We need a way of getting to Simmersville without being detected. Any ideas?"

"It's fastest by air," said Patti.

"Maybe," said Gügor, scratching his chin, "there's a way we could use Jean-Remy's flying pan."

Patti sighed. "Don't take this the wrong way, Gügor, but there ain't no way you'll fit in a flying pan, 'specially not with the rest of us along for the ride."

"Wait a minute," said Jean-Remy. He swooped down from where he had been perched, up on the railing of the Think Tank. "Gügor! You may be right!"

Harrumphrey eyed Jean-Remy suspiciously. "How big is this flying pan of yours?"

"*No-no-no!* Ze flying pan, it is too small. Too small to carry anything but ze perfect *crêpe! However*, ze technology I used to *make* ze flying pan, it was based on something else. Something . . . *top secret*." Jean-Remy looked at Harrumphrey. "I zink you know what it is I am talking about."

An odd grumbling noise came from deep inside Harrumphrey's throat. "Are you suggesting what I think you're suggesting?"

"Why not? It is a secret flight, no? Zis would be ze perfect time to test it!"

"Except no one in creaturedom has ever successfully piloted a machine like that. Not without crashing, at least."

"What machine?" asked Elliot. (This sounded very intriguing.)

"*Ze Coleopter-copter!*"

"Is that like a colonoscopy?" asked Leslie. "Grandpa Freddy had one of those last year. I don't think he liked it."

"No-no-no. *Ze Coleopter-copter!*"

"I think you mean *chiropractor*," said Elliot. "But isn't that like a crazy masseuse? I don't see how that'll help us—"

"*No! No! No!*" cried Jean-Remy. He took a moment to catch his breath. Then he spoke each syllable very slowly. "Now listen. *KOH . . . LEE . . . OP . . . TER . . . COP . . . TER.* Come. We will show you."

Patti, Jean-Remy, and Harrumphrey led Elliot and Leslie deeper into the laboratory. They were taken through a small, nondescript door that emerged into yet another warehouse-like space even bigger than the cavernous laboratory they had just left. Once again, the children were reminded of the impossible dimensions of a building built with creature physics.

"We have a prototype stored in here," said Patti, "but Harrumphrey's right. None of us have the know-how—or the guts—to fly it."

"What prototype?" asked Leslie. "Where is it? This just looks like a deserted airplane hangar."

"An airplane hangar, yes," said Jean-Remy. "Zat is a good comparison. But it is not deserted." He flitted to the wall and tapped an intricate combination into a wall-mounted view-screen.

After a moment's silence, the floor began to tremble.

Leslie grabbed Elliot's arm. "What's happening?"

"*Watch,*" said Harrumphey, "and stand back."

Before their eyes, a vast spiral of blue light, as broad as an Olympic-sized swimming pool, glowed on the floor. The lines of the spiral broadened and separated as a massive circle opened up to reveal . . . *nothing*. There was nothing there but a vast darkness. Leslie squeezed Elliot's arm. They sensed they were staring into the most bottomless of bottomless pits. They swayed on their feet. They felt dizzy. Dimly flickering stars appeared before their eyes.

Stars!

Those weren't sparkles of dizziness floating before their eyes. They were *actual stars*! Staring into the darkness below them, Elliot and Leslie saw the glitter and swirl of countless distant suns.

Elliot was breathless. "You've got a whole universe down there!"

Harrumphrey chuckled. "Not even close. Barely enough room for a galaxy! Maybe two, in a pinch."

"A *g-galaxy?*" Elliot stammered. He tried (and failed) to stifle the quaver in his voice.

"But of course!" said Jean-Remy. "Down zere is where we keep our *very biggest* inventions!"

"Inventions . . . like w-what?" asked Leslie.

"Like ze Coleopter-copter!" said Jean-Remy. Again, his tiny fingers danced across the glowing controls, and suddenly, the stars began to vanish. Something was blotting them out, rising to the surface of the empty circle. It was *something huge*.

"Look," said Leslie. "It's . . . it's a . . . it's a . . ."

"*A beetle!*" cried Elliot.

It was an enormous insect, its huge body covered with emerald-green forewings, veined with streaks of yellow. The head was entirely black, with two enormous horns protruding from the upper and lower jaws, one on top of the other. The upper horn was largest, looming forward nearly as long as the rest of its body. It curved up and then down to a pointed tip, while the lower horn arced upward to meet it at two-thirds its length. On either side of the head, at the point where the horns connected, were its eyes—shining, impassive, and dark.

For a moment, Elliot and Leslie were stunned. They expected the enormous creature to crawl off the rising platform and gobble them up. But the giant beetle didn't move. Then they saw why.

"It's not alive," said Elliot. "It's a machine."

It took a bit of squinting to make out the rivets that speckled its metal skin, and the huge gears hidden in the shadows of its mouth. In fact, it looked like a beetle in every respect but one. *It was huge.* Jean-Remy had been serious when he called this place an *airplane* hangar. The beetle was the size of a jet fighter!

The platform supporting the monstrous insect locked into place. The Coleopter-copter rocked gently on its three pairs of improbably narrow legs, all of them barbed with claws at each joint. The whirlpool once again vanished under the floor, and the room returned to an eerie silence—even more eerie than before, thanks to the incredible mechanical beast that stood before them.

"Elliot, Leslie," said Harrumphery. "Meet Hercules, our newest flying machine."

Elliot snapped his fingers. "Hercules! Of course! As in *Hercules beetle*, the biggest of them all!"

"Precisely," said Harrumphrey. "*Coleoptera* is the scientific name for the order of insects commonly known as beetles."

"So," said Leslie, "what you're saying is you built a

jetliner-sized beetle that lives in a glowing galaxy and that no one can pilot because it's too dangerous to fly?"

Harrumphrey nodded. "That about sums it up."

"And what made you think," Leslie went on, "this was a good way to get to Simmersville *without being noticed*?"

Patti shrugged as if that was the easiest question anyone had asked all day. "Because it's undetectable," she said.

"Undetectable?!" Elliot spluttered. *"It's gigantic!"*

"Also," Leslie added, "shaped like a beetle."

"It's the craziest flying machine ever," Elliot protested. "How could anyone miss it?"

"Quite easily, in fact," said Patti, "thanks to my design. The underbelly is camouflaged to look like the night sky. The onboard computers record what's above it and then project it across the bottom. It could be flying right over your heads and you'd never know it!"

"And what about radar?" asked Elliot. "It's sure to pick you up."

"Actually, no," said Jean-Remy. "Zat is precisely ze reason we built it. A Coleopter-copter is utterly invisible to radar!"

"That's impossible!"

"Exactly," said Harrumphrey, "which is why it works. You see, what not a lot of people know about computers is that they come with a keen sense of the impossible." Harrumphey spread his stumpy legs and thrust out his chin. It was the professorial posture he took whenever explaining the trickier concepts of creature science. "We creatures, on the other hand, we've known about the Computational Plausibility Field for years. In a nutshell, computers are only as good as what they *believe*. For example, you know when you get one of those error messages? 'Illegal operation,' it says and up pops the 'fail whale.'

This usually happens because you've asked your computer to do something it just doesn't believe is possible. Or, to use the more technical term, you've 'ruptured its Plausibility Field.' You've asked it to do something, but—even if that thing may be *theoretically possible*—the computer's thinking, 'What do you take me for? A wristwatch with a calculator?' What you see is the error message, but believe me—that's really what the computer's thinking. You'd be surprised how skeptical they can be. And the same goes for radar systems, which are basically just computers with ears. Oh, sure, they can detect *all kinds* of things. But what if they detect something they just don't believe in—like, say a two-hundred-foot mechanical beetle that flies by opening a set of gigantic elytra and flapping its inner wings? Lemme tell you, when radar picks up something like that, *it blows that radar's mind*. Boom! You see what I mean?"

"Barely," said Leslie.

Elliot sighed. "I think you just ruptured *my* Plausibility Field."

"Trust me, it works. The only problem," Harrumphrey explained, "is that we don't have anyone who can fly it."

"Oh, I wouldn't worry about that!" called a voice from the hangar entrance.

It was Reggie.

Elliot and the others peeked back into the laboratory and saw the blubbery bombastadon scaling up a great heap of old equipment that was pushed off in one corner.

"Reggie?" asked Jean-Remy. "What are you doing?"

At first, Elliot and Leslie thought Reggie was scaling nothing more than a pile of old junk. Then they spotted the very comfortable-looking chair at the top of the heap.

"That's the teleporter prototype," said Elliot, "isn't it?"

"It *is*," said the professor, rushing across the laboratory to join them, "and Reggie, you of all people should know it isn't working properly. It still sends everything to Antarctica!"

"Precisely!" Reggie lowered his great bombastadon bottom into the second-most comfortable chair in the universe. "That is the very place I intend to go."

"What? Right now?"

"Of course! I know just the fellow we need."

"Just the fellow we need for what?"

"To pilot your flying machine, of course."

Before the professor could ask who Reggie had in mind, there was a great blue crack of electricity, and Colonel-Admiral Reggie T. Pusslegut was *ZZZZAPPED* into nothing but a puff of smoke.

CHAPTER 6

In which Cosmo Clutch (almost) sets a record

Cosmo Clutch looked over the edge of the iceberg. It was a long way down. (It was *always* a long way down.) He was about to set the new Antarctic record for Greatest Distance Traveled in an Unpowered Ice-Glider. He had already set seemingly unbeatable records for Fastest Pole-to-Pole Voyage in a Trans-Dimensional Zeppelin, Highest Altitude Achieved on a Pedal-Powered Flying Machine, Ice-Speed Record for Fastest Downhill Run on a Rocket Sledge, and many others. But in all his years of daredevilry, he had never attempted a record in an unpowered ice-glider. Anyone else would have been trembling in their boots, but not Cosmo Clutch. He never trembled for anything.

On the far side of the gorge, he could make out his awaiting fans. He took out his pocket mirror and held it up to his face. It was important to make sure there was nothing stuck in his teeth. After all, once he had set the record, the press photographers would want their pictures. *Lots* of pictures.

After picking some straw from between his incisors, Cosmo turned the mirror sideways to check his profile. He looked good (as always). His snout still had the leanness of youth, his antlers were polished to a high shine, and his eyes sparkled with the steely gleam his fans expected.

Perfect!

He turned to face his ice-glider. It sat silently in its launcher, the largest slingshot in all of creaturedom. (To be honest, calling it a "glider" was generous. It was little more than an icicle the size of a sofa. Once it was shot out of the launcher, however, it would become so much more. It would become his one-way ticket to posterity!)

Cosmo checked the winches, the pulleys, the springs, and the extremely elastic bands that would propel him across the gorge like an arrow. Just to be sure he'd make it all the way, he had pulled them back significantly farther than he had ever pulled them back before.

He donned his helmet. It was bright red, perfectly round, and so fiercely waxed it shone like the sun. Moreover, it had been specially designed for him by a bespoke haberdasher in Greenland. Two slots had been cut out of the helmet so his antlers could comfortably stick out on either side. When he slipped it on, he knew he was ready.

A voice crackled over his walkie-talkie. "Mr. Clutch?" It was the official from the *Creature Book of World Records*. "We're ready on this side. What about you?"

Cosmo responded with a phrase he had believed all his life: "I was born ready."

He made one last check of the glider's parachute mechanism. It would deploy on final descent and allow him to gently touch down on the far side of the gorge. After that, there was only one thing to do: He climbed aboard the icicle (or rather, the "ice-glider").

He strapped himself in and used the slingshot's calibrators to account for air temperature and wind speed. Then, using his feet, he pushed the massive elastic one inch farther back. (Just in case.)

"Countdown from ten," Cosmo spoke into his walkie-talkie.

"Roger that."

"Ten . . . nine . . . eight . . . seven . . ."

Cosmo dug his heels into the ice-glider's stirrups.

". . . six . . . five . . . four . . ."

Cosmo narrowed his eyes.

". . . three . . . two . . ."

Cosmo picked his teeth one last time. (Just in case.)

"One!"

The sudden blast of speed made Cosmo gasp. Not in fear, but because the slingshot had whisked him into the air so fast, the sudden change of pressure sucked the air from his lungs. For an instant, there was a silence so profound he thought he might have been knocked unconscious, but then came a thunderous whoosh of air, and Cosmo Clutch knew he was on his way.

The Antarctic sea spread out below him, vast ice sheets extending in every direction. It was quite beautiful. That was when it all went wrong.

His first clue was an unsettling dampness between his legs. At first, he assumed he had wet himself out of sheer excitement. Then he realized the source of his soggy bottom was something much more alarming: The ice-glider was melting! But how? It wasn't possible. Unless . . .

He slapped one palm to the shiny red forehead of his custom-made helmet. *Friction*, he thought. Air speed. He was going too fast! How could he have been so stupid?! *Why-why-WHY* had he put that extra bit of tension in the elastic bands?! (Because he wanted to make it to the other side, of course.) But now look what was happening!

Nevertheless, he didn't lose his cool. He gazed calmly left and right and saw the leading edge of both wings were melting, sagging and dripping away to nothing. Meanwhile, down between his legs, the fuselage had shrunk to the size of a small pony.

Then the size of a coffee table.

Then the size of a pillow.

Then the size of a pop bottle.

Then the size of a toothpick.

Then . . .

Nothing.

All that remained of the ice-glider was an embarrassingly drenched pair of pants.

Cosmo Clutch, the greatest daredevil record-breaker in all of creaturedom (or so he claimed), was soaring through the Antarctic air with nothing to hold him up but a flak jacket, a shiny red helmet, and the mad flapping of his own two arms.

"Well," he said to himself, "I guess this is it." He tried to appear debonair as he sailed over the crowd of screaming fans, flashbulbs popping as he went. He was traveling so fast, he overshot the target completely. In no time, he was flailing over nothing but an empty field of snow and ice.

Then Cosmo Clutch saw something he didn't expect: a bombastadon. He was dressed in high-ranking military garb, his saber rattling as he scampered across the ice field. Where had he come from? Cosmo was sure there hadn't been a bombastadon there a moment ago. After all, they were difficult to miss against the endless white of Antarctica. This one was waving his arms and shouting something. Cosmo couldn't hear him, of course; he was too high up. But that was about to change.

"*Geronimoooo!*" screamed Cosmo Clutch, soaring down into the soft, blubbery arms of—

FWWWHUMP!

"Pusslegut, is that you?"

Reggie nodded. "Another record attempt, I see. Good man!"

"Wouldn't call it good, myself," Cosmo told his old friend. "Wouldja believe the darn thing melted on me up there?"

Reggie released one arm and set Cosmo down on the ice. "I'm sure next time you'll succeed with flying colors. See what I did? *Flying* colors! Ho-ho!"

Cosmo sighed. He had forgotten about the Colonel-Admiral's dippy sense of humor. "If I *do* ever succeed, I'll owe it all to you for catching me today. If there's any way I can repay the favor, you go ahead and let me know."

"In fact," said Reggie, "there is something I have in mind."

"You name it."

"Well, Old Clutchie, I was just wondering . . . have you ever flown a beetle before?"

 TELELECTRIC PENCIL

CHAPTER 7

In which Elliot discovers that some buildings are even stranger than the ones in which his uncle works

On the way home from DENKi-3000 Headquarters, Elliot wondered what his parents would say when he asked to spend the weekend in Simmersville, with Leslie and her mother. He certainly didn't want to mention the food festival. They might get the wrong impression. They might think he was taking an interest in their work as food critics. That would be a disaster! But he *definitely* couldn't tell them why he was really going. His parents had a habit of screwing up their faces whenever he mentioned Uncle Archie.

As it turned out, none of this mattered. When he arrived home, his parents were waiting for him.

"Elliot!" cried his mother. "We're *so* glad you're home!"

"You are?" Something fishy was going on. Elliot could tell.

"Of course we are, son," said his father. "We've got some big news for you."

"Actually," Elliot started, "I have some news mysel—"

"No time for that now. Look at this!" His father flipped open the morning's copy of the *Bickleburgh Bugle*, opening it to the food section. A bright full-page advertisement blazed across the page:

THIS SATURDAY!
COME FOR THE FOOD!
COME FOR THE DRINK!
STAY FOR THE WORLD-FAMOUS
DINNER-THEATRE-STYLE
COSTUME CABARET!
THIS YEAR FEATURING THE AMAZING
BORIS MINOR AND THE KARLOFFS!
THE SIMMERSVILLE ANNUAL
FOOD FESTIVAL!
A FEAST FOR ALL THE SENSES!
"The must-do, must-chew event of the year!"

—Peter & Marjorie von Doppler, "Chew on This."

Elliot's mother cleared her throat. "Now, Elliot, before you say anything, I want to explain. We know you aren't keen on following in the family footsteps and becoming a restaurant critic, but you really ought to consider it."

"Honestly, son," said his father. "How could you *not* want to have your own nationally syndicated food column? Best job in the world, the way I see it! You eat the finest meals around, and then you write about them. *And* you never have to worry about too many adjectives! How about that? Is there any better way to make a living?"

Elliot was about to answer this obviously rhetorical question by saying, "Yes. *Inventing stuff.*" But he didn't think this was a good idea.

"That's why we'd like you to have a look at this." Elliot's mother waved the back of her hand over the advertisement. "It's the Simmersville Annual—"

"I know all about it," said Elliot.

His parents gasped. "You do?!"

Elliot pointed to the DINNER-THEATRE-STYLE COSTUME CABERET! line. "There's a bunch of song-and-dance numbers at the end, right?"

His mother's face brightened and she spluttered, "Y-yes! Th-th-that's right!"

Elliot could hardly blame her for being so surprised. This was probably the first time he had shown interest in his parents' jobs at the newspaper. He liked food as much as anyone, but beyond cooking it and eating it (both of which he considered worthy pursuits), *writing about it* just seemed silly.

"The *Bugle* is sending your mother and me on a special assignment to cover the festival, and we'd like you to join us."

"Actually," said Elliot, "that's exactly what—"

His father held up one hand for Elliot to stop speaking. "Before you say no, before you tell us you'd rather sleep over at a friend's house, or *worse*, spend the weekend with Uncle Archie, I want to remind you this isn't a choice. You're coming with us whether you like it or not."

"Don't worry," said his mother. "Just wait until you see the Dinner-Theatre-Style Costume Cabaret! I just know you're going to love it!"

* * *

On Friday evening, Elliot, Leslie, and their parents set off for Simmersville. Since they were all headed to the same place, Elliot opted to travel with Leslie and her mother. In the backseat of the Fangs' rusty red Volkswagen, Elliot and Leslie whispered about how they would meet up with Uncle Archie and the others once they arrived.

Famous Freddy's big white trailer was hitched behind the car, bumping and bounding along the highway. It was packed with ingredients and banners and all the cooking equipment Leslie's mother would need to set up a stall in the Simmersville market square. In the front seat, Leslie's mother mumbled to herself as she drove. From the moment they set off, she had been muttering nonstop.

"What's she saying?" Elliot asked, whispering to Leslie.

"She's reciting the recipes aloud. It helps her remember."

"Has she forgotten them?"

Leslie shook her head. "It's more that she's only just learned them. Back at the restaurant, she has all of Grandpa Freddy's old cookbooks, but at the festival she won't have time to look anything up." Leslie looked at the back of her mother's head, at the dark hair falling past her shoulders. "I told her not to worry, but she wouldn't listen."

"*I'd* be worried if I were her!" said Elliot.

"I heard that, Elliot," said Leslie's mother. "You're not helping."

Elliot lowered his voice again. "She'll have to cook for *hundreds* of people and she won't even have your grandfather to help."

"Mom said exactly the same thing, but I think she *will* have his help." Leslie opened her bag and took out a crinkled old newspaper article. Elliot was surprised to see it was from the food section of a newspaper, but not from the *Bickleburgh Bugle*. This page had come from the *Simmersville Tribune*. The article featured a large photograph of Leslie's grandfather and the headline read, **Bickleburgh Chef Sets New Record.**

Leslie pointed to the first lines of the article. "Grandpa Freddy has attended every single food fest since they first began!"

"So you think he'll be there."

"He *has* to be! If he doesn't go, he could lose the record. And this is Grandpa Freddy we're talking about—*Famous* Freddy. If I know him like I think I know him, he'll be there."

Leslie's mother stopped murmuring again. "I thought I told you," she said. "Stop worrying about your grandfather. Wherever he is, I'm sure he's fine!"

"But what if he isn't?" asked Leslie.

"He can take care of himself," said her mother, and returned to another mumbled recipe.

After they'd driven two hours on the highway, a huge sign loomed up beside the road. The edges were painted with all kinds of food, everything from apples, avocados, and bagels down to yams, yogurt, and zucchini cupcakes. Smack in the middle of it all, it said, **Welcome to Simmersville!**

The town was smaller than Bickleburgh and much older. There were cobblestone streets, painted wooden fences, and crooked houses. Even though much of the place was old and faded and many of the buildings were beginning to crumble and sag, Elliot thought there was something charming about Simmersville. Maybe even beautiful.

"Sort of reminds me of the old mansion where Uncle Archie works," he said.

"If that's true," said Leslie, "then this whole town must be full of hidden doors and secret passages."

As they reached the crest of a hill, three very different buildings appeared. They rose abruptly, fifteen or twenty stories high. Unlike almost everything else in Simmersville, they were made of steel and glass. This part of the city reminded them of the rest of DENKi-3000: strange, modern, incongruous buildings, shooting up from the center of town. Much to Elliot's surprise, however, these three buildings were *even stranger* than the ones back in Bickleburgh.

"Is that *a fork*?" asked Elliot, pointing to the middle tower.

"Yep, and on either side is a knife and a spoon," said Leslie, referring to the other two towers.

Leslie's mother glanced back at Elliot. "You've really never heard of the Heppleworth buildings?"

"Not really," said Elliot, though he had to admit the buildings were impressive. He wondered if, living all his life in Bickleburgh and obsessing over his uncle's work at DENKi-3000, there were bits of the world he had missed out on.

"Here we are." Leslie's mother took a sharp turn down a narrow street, and the Heppleworth towers vanished behind a row of houses.

They bumped toward the center of town until they came to their hotel, the Simmersville Inn. It was built on the edge of the famous market square. From the parking lot, they could see the square was filled with workers, erecting stalls and putting up banners in preparation for the festival.

The Simmersville Inn was made of rough white stone and had four floors. When they went inside, they were greeted by the clerk. Although *greeted* wasn't quite the right word. For a hotel clerk, this woman seemed unusually shy. Although her face was plump and pleasant, with her blonde hair tied back with an emerald-green ribbon, her posture was all wrong. She was cowering in the corner behind the reception desk, hugging herself with her arms. When she said, "Welcome to the

Simmersville Inn," it came out as inaudibly as the mumbled recipes of Leslie's mother.

"We're here for the festival," said Leslie, running up to the counter.

The clerk came forward with a couple of pages of paperwork. Her name tag said: **My name is Emily**. Oddly, the whole time Emily dealt with Leslie's mother, the clerk kept her elbows stiffly pressed into her ribs. She looked very uncomfortable.

"What name is it under?" she asked.

"Fang," said Leslie's mother. "Jennifer Fang and—*oh*! I forgot my bag in the car." She chuckled. "My head's obviously too full of recipes for anything else!" She ran out to fetch her purse.

The girl behind the counter smiled weakly. "You guys've got nice rooms," she told them. "Top floor. Great views of the square." She sidled along the counter to a cupboard on the wall. It was full of keys, hanging on hooks. When she reached up to retrieve the ones for Elliot and Leslie, the sleeve of the girl's shirt slid up her arm—and there was something very strange about it: *It was the wrong color.* The skin under the girl's sleeve was scaly, like a snake's, and nearly as green as the ribbon in her hair!

Emily hastily tugged her sleeve back into place as Leslie and Elliot looked at each other with almost identical expressions of shock. *Did you see that?* Elliot mouthed. Leslie nodded—just as her mother came jogging back into the lobby with her purse.

Following close behind were Elliot's parents, who had just arrived themselves. As soon as both families were checked in, everyone agreed that over the long drive they had all worked up an appetite.

"In that case, we're all in for a special treat," said Elliot's father, smacking his lips.

"Oh, yes!" Elliot's mother agreed. "The restaurant here at the Simmersville Inn *is famous*!"

The children were ushered toward the restaurant before they could ask about the clerk's strange green-skinned arm. What could it possibly mean? Before they rounded the corner, Elliot looked back one last time, but the girl was gone. The only thing he saw was the door behind the desk, shutting with a quiet *click*.

CHAPTER 8

In which Elliot orders "the Special," Leslie orders a cheese sandwich, and their parents register a formal complaint

The restaurant at the Simmersville Inn was called The Smiling Mudsucker. It was quite fancy. Filigreed light fixtures threw dim light over the plush furniture and pristine white tablecloths.

"What's a mudsucker?" asked Leslie, as they were shown to their table.

"A kind of fish," Elliot's mother answered. "They're famous for their seafood here. See what I mean?" She pointed to a monstrous aquarium dominating the rear of the restaurant. It filled the full width of the room and was so deep you couldn't see the other side. The water behind the glass simply faded into darkness. Inside, the aquarium teemed with life, not just with fish but other things too, strange sea life like nothing they had ever seen.

"Looks like an aquatic Creature Department in there," Leslie whispered.

Tentacles, teeth, spiny fins, and shimmering scales glowed and bubbled behind the glass. Some of the creatures were quite large. They could make out huge shapes, undulating in the shadows, lost behind colorful curtains of fish. One of those huge shapes swam forward.

It looked like a cross between a turtle, a lobster, and a starfish. It had the head, wrinkly neck, and hard shell of a turtle, while its legs (five of them) resembled the pebbled orange limbs of a starfish. Then there were its hands, which couldn't really be called hands since they were large, crab-like pincers.

The creature undulated its many legs, propelling itself in an elegant loop on the other side of the glass. Countless schools of fish skittered away to give the creature space before it swooped back and vanished into the shadows.

"I hope *that's* not on the menu," said Leslie's mother.

"Don't worry," said Elliot's father. "The aquarium is only for atmosphere." He looked at Elliot. "Take note, son. *Atmosphere* is the most important part of any good restaurant."

"Atmosphere?" asked Elliot. "What about *the food*?"

His mother tousled his hair. "Oh, Elliot! We have so much to teach you!"

Whoever said I wanted to learn? Elliot thought.

The waiter approached their table. He was a thin man in a tuxedo so sharply pressed it looked as if his lapels might lop off the tips of your fingers. He stood haughtily straight and held his head high, his shiny nose poking up in the air.

"Are you ready to order?"

Elliot's father nodded eagerly. "I'll have the *huitlacoche* and sturgeon ravioli, please."

"What's that supposed to be?" asked Elliot, making a face.

His mother kicked him under the table.

"*Ow!*"

"I'll have the cuttlefish and quail-egg quiche," she said.

If the waiter was impressed with these choices, he didn't show it. He responded merely by sniffing the air with his upturned nose.

Elliot felt his parents turn their faces expectantly toward him. But Elliot couldn't think about food. He was too preoccupied with the *real* reason he had come to Simmersville: to find out what the ghorks were up to, and to rescue Jean-Remy's sister!

"*Ahem!*" said the waiter, cutting into Elliot's thoughts. "Would you prefer if I recommended something?"

Elliot felt a surge of relief. "Oh, yes, please!"

The waiter rolled his eyes in disappointment (perhaps even with a modicum of disgust).

"*The Special!*" he announced. His finger came down with a thud, nailing Elliot's menu to the table. It had landed on a square of frilly white paper that had been glued hastily to the bottom of the menu's final page. Typed on this slip of paper was:

THE SPECIAL
A top-secret recipe created by our new head chef.

Elliot wasn't sure this was what he wanted for dinner. "How come there's no description?" he asked.

The waiter moved his finger to tap the words *top secret*— THUD, THUD. "I'm sure it's excellent," he said. "I'm told the new chef is a genius."

"Hear that, son?" Elliot's father slapped him on the back. "A genius!"

"Yes," said the waiter, turning only slightly to face Elliot's father, "and it must be true, because you know how *they* are. Eccentric! This one refuses to remove his costume for the big cabaret tomorrow, so he *must* be a genius."

Elliot sighed. He had never ordered something without

knowing what it was, but his parents looked so hopeful and expectant, and besides, The and Special were just about the only words on the menu he could read.

"Fine," he said at last. "I'll have it. The Special."

The whole time the waiter spoke, Leslie had been staring at the kitchen doors. "This new head chef?" she asked the waiter. "Does he happen to be an old man? Skinny, Asian, completely bald? With a smiling face and sort of bad posture?"

The waiter thrust out his lower lip. "How would I know? He never takes off his costume."

"Costume," Leslie whispered. "I wonder . . ."

Her mother reached over and stroked Leslie's arm. "Please, Leslie, stop worrying. Grandpa Freddy's going to be fine. Why don't you go ahead and order."

Leslie squinted up at the waiter. "Do you do grilled cheese sandwiches?"

"Grilled?! Cheese?!" He was obviously appalled.

"Actually," said Leslie's mother, "that sounds good. I haven't had grilled cheese in ages! Especially not gourmet grilled cheese."

"That's because there's no such thing," said the waiter.

Leslie's mother clapped the menu shut. "Two grilled cheese sandwiches, please!"

The waiter sighed. "I'll see what I can do."

Elliot looked at his parents. "Um . . . can I have grilled cheese, too?"

They responded in unison. "NO!"

The waiter left in a huff. Before long he returned with five plates of food. The dishes Elliot's parents had ordered looked colorful and inviting. On the other hand, the two grilled cheese sandwiches seemed to be deliberately wilted and pathetic: four triangles of white bread, oozing orange sludge onto an otherwise bare plate.

Elliot, meanwhile, was presented with an elegant platter covered by a silver dome. The waiter lifted it off the plate with the flourish.

"*The Special!*" he announced.

Everyone at the table screamed.

"AAIIIEEEEEEGH!"

That was because it looked like Elliot's dinner was about to *eat him.*

"W-w-what is this?" Elliot spluttered.

"It's an homage to our hallowed name," the waiter explained. "The Smiling Mudsucker!"

Elliot's dinner was arranged on the plate to resemble an enormous mouth. Vegetable lips were drawn back in a malicious smirk. They revealed soft pink gums carved from rare roast beef. Triangles of bread and cheese were meticulously arranged like rows of jagged fangs. Finally, a tongue of bright red salmon flopped across the plate, glistening with buttery saliva.

"Bon appétit!" said the waiter, before returning to the kitchen.

Elliot stared at what had to be the ghastliest dish ever served. And it wasn't just ghastly, it was oddly lifelike.

"If that thing moves," Elliot whispered, "I'm not eating it."

But the dish sat perfectly still, and (eventually) everyone at the table relaxed enough to begin the meal. It was quickly apparent, however, that although the food looked impressive (in its own unusual way), it *tasted awful.* Or rather, it didn't taste of anything.

"I'm beginning to wish I'd gone with a cheese sandwich!" said Elliot's father.

"You're not missing anything," said Leslie's mother, screwing up her face. "If this is gourmet grilled cheese, then I'm the vice president of Ecuador!"

"*Ugh!* This is unacceptable!" Elliot's mother threw down

her napkin and pushed out her chair. The other two adults did the same, and a moment later, all three were marching into the kitchen to register their complaints with the chef.

Alone at the table with Leslie, Elliot looked down at his plate. He had eaten only a few bites of his so-called Special. Much of the disturbing mouth remained, grinning ferociously up at him. "Does this remind you of something?" he asked Leslie, pointing to the plate.

"A great white shark?"

"I was thinking of something more specific. Actually, some-one more specific. Don't you think it looks a lot like—"

CRASH!

The clang and rattle of pots, pans, and smashing plates erupted from the kitchen.

"*WHAT?!*" boomed a voice from inside. "How *dare* you?! You think I ain't got good taste?! *TASTE?!* There ain't nobody in the *whole world* who knows more about TASTE than me!"

Elliot and Leslie looked at each other. They looked down at Elliot's plate. At that moment, in each of their heads, something clicked. They *knew* that mouth. They knew that *voice*. It was—

"*AAIIIEEEEEEEEGH!*"

Leslie's mother and Elliot's parents came barreling out of the kitchen.

"Run!" they shouted.

"The new chef!"

"He's gone berserk!"

It was true. Hot on their heels, chasing them out of the kitchen, was precisely the person—or rather, *the ghork*—Elliot and Leslie had heard.

"*Grinner!*"

CHAPTER 9

In which a tablecloth is put to good use,
the festivalgoers think it's all part of the fun,
and Grinner reveals a taste for leather

Grinner, leader of all the mouth-ghorks of creature-dom, was dressed in chef's whites and a matching toque. Over his head he brandished an enormous wooden spoon, big as a baseball bat. Leslie's mother and Elliot's parents raced past the aquarium, rainbows of fish streaming behind the glass like speed lines in a comic strip.

"Chef, stop! You're scaring the customers!" The impeccably dressed waiter burst out of the kitchen. He tried grabbing Grinner's arm, but the big ghork was too fast.

Grinner plucked the waiter up by the scruff of his tux. "Quiet, twerp," he said. "Back to work!" With a casual swing of his arm, he tossed the poor man back into the kitchen. He tumbled through the doors to a resounding clatter of pots and pans. All of this happened so quickly Elliot and Leslie could only watch in shock.

Grinner leapt over a table and cornered the adults in front of the aquarium. "Now then," he sneered. "Who wants to go into tomorrow's special?"

"Yo, bigmouth!" Leslie shouted at Grinner from the table. "Remember us?"

Grinner paused, the wooden spoon raised above his head.

Elliot pointed an accusing finger at him. "I've had better food in the hospital!"

"Prepare to be poached, you little creeps!" Grinner took a step toward the children, but while his back was turned, their parents had slung a white tablecloth in front of his leg. When Grinner went to move, they tightened it.

"What the—?"

Grinner tripped head over heels and smashed one of the tables to splinters.

"Now's your chance, you two!" shouted Leslie's mother. "*Run!*"

Elliot and Leslie sprinted out of the restaurant. Behind them, they heard their parents wrestling with Grinner. Unfortunately, two food critics and a short-order cook were no match for an angry ghork. He kicked off the tablecloth and threw it over the adults. In seconds, he had them swaddled and knotted up in the same white fabric they had used to trip him up.

Elliot and Leslie rushed out into the market square, already milling with people. They cast curious glances at the two pan-icking children, racing out of the old hotel.

"Look out, everybody!" Elliot shouted at them. "There's a ghork coming—and he's right behind us!"

"A what?" asked a gray-haired old woman.

"One of those!" Elliot told her, pointing to Grinner, who came bounding out of the lobby, swinging his wooden spoon like a club.

"Dearie me," said the old woman, hardly raising an eyebrow.

"They've certainly spared no expense on costumes this year."

Leslie waved her arms at the woman. "It's *not* a costume! That's a *real ghork*!"

"Ghork?" The old lady chuckled. "What a silly word! These cabarets get more ridiculous every year!"

"*Ugh!*" Leslie gave up trying to convince the woman. She and Elliot dashed for the far side of the square. Over there, the old brick buildings were packed closely together, making narrow alleyways where they hoped they could escape.

Sadly, just like the old woman, everyone else thought the green-skinned, saliva-spewing ogre was nothing more than a prelude to the big Dinner-Theatre-Style Costume Cabaret that would cap off the festival. They were even helpful enough (at least for Grinner) to clear a path for him. Some of them even clapped.

Elliot couldn't believe it. "They're leading him straight to us!"

They reached the far side of the square and ran into an alley, turning left and right at random in hopes of giving Grinner the slip. At first, it seemed to be working. The sound of the ghork's pounding footsteps faded behind them. Around another corner they found a row of recycling bins. They were arranged side-by-side and set apart from the wall, leaving just enough space for Elliot and Leslie to hide.

"I think he gave up," Elliot whispered.

"Maybe."

"Why was he cooking in that restaurant?"

Leslie wrinkled her nose. "Can you call that cooking?"

"No, but I thought the ghorks had taken over the Heppleworth Food factory, not some—"

Elliot stopped mid-sentence. He heard something. It wasn't

the shouting, the growling, the pounding feet they had heard pursuing them across the square. This was something else. It was a sound in three parts: 1) shuffling footsteps; 2) an odd slurping sound; and 3) the sound of coughing and spitting. Then the noises repeated.

Shuffle . . .

Slurp . . .

Splutter . . .

"Is that him?" Elliot asked.

"I don't know, but whatever it is, it's coming closer."

They crawled out of their hiding place to keep going, but around the next corner, there was only a dead end. There was nowhere to run. They could only sneak back behind the recycling bins and hope they went unnoticed.

Peering out through a gap between the bins, they kept their eyes on the glow at the end of the alley. The sound was very close now.

Shuffle . . .

Slurp . . .

Splutter . . .

"It's almost here," Leslie whispered.

A moment later, a shadowy figure blotted out the light at the end of the alley. It was a beast the size of an enormous hound, maybe even a small horse. It loped on all fours, head bowed low to the pavement. When it stalked into the alleyway, however, they saw it wasn't an animal at all. It was Grinner. The mouthghork was crawling on his hands and knees. Then Leslie and Elliot saw the reason his head was so close to the ground.

"He's *licking* it!" Leslie whispered in disgust.

They now saw the shuffling noise was Grinner's awkward

crawling; the slurps were the slither of his pale, snake-like tongue; and the splutter came when he shook his head from side to side, spraying his filthy saliva across the walls. Pebbles and dirt and scraps of trash hit the bricks and stuck, glued there with his slimy spit.

"*Gross*," Elliot whispered.

"I know you're down there," Grinner growled. "I can *taste* it! The girl's wearing saddle shoes. Quality leather soles! And the boy. You're in . . ." He slobbered his tongue across the pavement. "A pair of casual loafers? What kind of kid wears casual loafers?" He smacked his lips and laughed. "Heh! You've got the *sole* of an old geezer! Get it? *Bwah-hah-hah-hah!*"

Leslie rolled her eyes. "His sense of humor's even worse than his cooking," she whispered.

But for Elliot, Grinner's joke was more than just an awful pun. The soul of an old geezer? Could it be true? A dorky twelve-year-old on the outside, a dorky *hundred*-and-twelve-year-old on the inside? *No*, he thought, *that wasn't true*. He knew he was *different* on the inside, but he wasn't some old fogey!

"A lot of people think it's them nose-ghorks who're the best trackers," Grinner said, his voice echoing up the alley. "But that's 'cuz they all underestimate *taste*. If only they were brave enough to bend over and taste the trail! Then they'd know the truth!"

There was something terrifying about Grinner's description of tracking by taste. It was frightening out of sheer repulsiveness, but far worse was how hopeless it made Elliot and Leslie feel. How could you escape a pursuer so intent on finding you, he was willing to crawl along the street, *licking your trail*?

"The taste down this alley is particularly . . . *fresh*." Grinner stroked his tongue languorously over the pavement one last time, then he leapt to his feet and bounded up the alley.

From their hiding place, Leslie and Elliot saw nothing but a great slavering mouth, roaring toward them through the darkness. It was horrifically pocked with endless teeth, each one dripping with muddy spit.

Elliot and Leslie huddled together in the shadows, hoping Grinner might run past them, but he didn't. He whacked away the recycling bins and revealed their hiding place.

"Well, well! Look what I found!"

Grinner hoisted them up by the backs of their shirts, just as he had done with the waiter at the Simmersville Inn. "The only question now is, Which one of you should I eat first?"

Leslie kicked out at him. "I hope you choke on my shinbone!"

Elliot wasn't sure antagonizing a hungry mouth-ghork was a good idea. Perhaps it would be better to stall. It might give them enough time to escape. Perhaps if he could get Grinner talking . . . "What is it with you ghorks?" he asked. "How come you keep trying to take over companies with secret Creature Departments? First DENKi-3000, now Heppleworth's Health Food."

"I'll bet they're jealous," Leslie said, catching on, "because all the other kinds of creatures can make cool stuff. All he can do is *lick the ground*."

"You just wait," Grinner told them. "We're cooking up something real special, so by the end of this dumb foodie festival, everyone in Simmersville is going to join us!"

"Why would anyone ever join up with the ghorks?"

Grinner smiled so hideously, Leslie shivered. "Because they won't have a choice," he said. "But I wouldn't worry about that. You won't be around to see it." He opened his mouth to reveal the soft wet flesh of his throat. "I've decided to eat you both at once!" He lifted them over his gaping maw and—

"*AAAIIIEEEEEEEGH!*"

It wasn't the children who screamed. It was Grinner. He screamed because, with his head thrown back, he was forced to gaze straight up into the night sky—*which had come to life*!

The stars shimmered and undulated like the flanks of some colossal fish. Suddenly, a monstrous black claw reached out of the night. It grabbed Grinner, just as he had grabbed Leslie and Elliot, by the scruff of his white uniform. He dropped the children, trying to fight free of the huge black pincers. It was no use. The terrified ghork was hefted off his feet and hauled into the sky.

"*AAAIIIEEEEEEEGH!*"

Leslie took a deep breath. "What was that?"

"Let's not stick around to find out."

Elliot grabbed her hand and they raced back toward the market square. Or so they hoped. They had made so many twists and turns to escape Grinner, they were now completely lost.

Then they saw it again. *The claw was back!* It poked out of the darkness, plucked them up like two specks of unwanted dust, and spirited them up, up, and away.

CHAPTER 10

In which the darkness is absolute, Gügor thinks ooey-gooey
is best, and Elliot and Leslie meet "Old Clutchie"

arkness comes in many flavors. There is the darkness of
climbing a rickety ladder and poking your head into a
musty attic. There is the darkness of walking through
a remote country field on a starless night. There is the darkness
of shutting your eyes just before bed. None of these, however, is
absolute darkness.

There is always that one tiny crack in the attic floorboards—
always the faint blue glow of the moon, straining through the
clouds—and even when you close your eyes, it's impossible to
escape the ghostly afterimage of what you were just looking at.
That's the funny thing about light. It always finds a way to slip
through the gaps.

But not this time.

"Elliot? Where are you?"

"I'm right here."

"Where's *here*?"

"How should I know? I can't see anything at all."

"Follow the sound of my voice."

Elliot tried, but Leslie's words echoed in all directions.

Behind the echoes he heard a strange thumping noise, like a great fist punching a gigantic soggy sponge—*ba-doom, ba-doom, ba-doom.* The noise muffled and confused the sound of Leslie's voice.

"Say something else," Elliot urged.

"Like what?"

"Anything."

"Once upon a time, there were these two kids who were suddenly picked up by a gigantic claw that came down out of the sky and . . . and . . . and I don't know what happened next because I can't see anything!"

"Was it just me," asked Elliot, "or did that gigantic flying claw look familiar?"

"Usually, I'd say no. Mostly because I don't run into gigantic flying claws all that much. But yes, I was thinking the same thing. Those were the same pincers on the front of that beetle-shaped-jet-fighter-flying-machine the creatures made."

"Hercules," said Elliot. "The Coleopter-copter."

"That's what I was thinking."

"But if we *are* inside him," said Elliot, "then where is everybody? And why is it so dark?"

"Oh, no," said Leslie.

"What is it?"

"What if something happened to them?"

"What do you mean?" Elliot asked.

"It picked up Grinner before us, so wouldn't that mean he's in here with us . . . somewhere?"

Elliot hadn't thought of that. "What if he's the one who turned out the lights?"

Suddenly, the floor veered sickeningly to one side, and they were thrown off balance, falling on their hands and knees.

"*Wah!*"

"*Oof!*"

"Wherever this is," said Elliot, "we're definitely still up in the air."

"*Ssh!* " Leslie hissed. "He might be listening."

They remained crouched on the floor, pressing their hands to the cold smoothness. They could almost feel the air, whistling past, just below their palms. They were afraid to climb back to their feet. The floor was too unsteady, and the darkness was—well, too dark. They crawled aimlessly in search of each other. The only sound was that persistent thumping noise. *Ba-doom, ba-doom, ba-doom* . . .

"Leslie?"

"Yeah?"

"Since we aren't sure what just happened, and since we don't really know where we are, and since we might be trapped inside the belly of a giant beetle with a hungry ghork . . . could I ask you a question?"

"Are you going to try and kiss me again because you think we're about to die?"

Elliot's stomach flipped. "*Ew!* No, it's nothing like that!"

"That's a relief," said Leslie. "So . . . what's the question?"

"I was just wondering, do you think my parents are weird?"

"*That's* what you want to ask me?"

"Well," said Elliot, "do you?"

Leslie told the truth. "No, I don't. But I understand if *you* do. I mean, I think my mom's *crazy* most of the time."

"She's just a bit strict, that's all."

"That's what I mean," said Leslie. "*You* think she's just a bit strict, and *I* think she's got a screw loose. It's the same with everyone. We all think our own parents are weirdos. That's why they're called parents. When you're a kid, it's just something you have to deal with. You know, love them in spite of their weirdness."

It might have been the absolute darkness, or the eerie thumping noise, or the fact that Leslie's voice seemed to come at him from everywhere at once, but Elliot sensed a certain wisdom in his friend's words. Nevertheless, he wasn't quite convinced.

"I guess," he said, "but my parents are *super* weird. Look how they acted at dinner. All they want to do is talk about food all day long. I feel like we're completely different people. Maybe even a completely different *species*."

"Everybody feels that way," said Leslie. "Sometimes."

"I feel that way *all* the time. I think . . . well, I just feel more comfortable around creatures."

"Maybe it's like your uncle's always saying: There's a little creature in everybody."

"Maybe sometimes," said Elliot, "there's more than a little."

There was another lull in their disembodied conversation, and Elliot once again considered the wisdom of Leslie's words.

"Maybe we'd better stop talking," he said. "If Grinner's in here—wherever *here* is—we don't want him finding us, right?"

Leslie didn't answer.

"Leslie?"

Again, there was no reply.

"Are you there?"

She wasn't. All Elliot heard was the insistent *ba-doom, ba-doom, ba-doom. . . .*

"*Leslie*, where are—"

"*Gotcha!*"

Elliot nearly wet himself. But it wasn't Grinner who grabbed him, it was Leslie! They gave each other a big hug.

"I didn't mean to scare you," she said, "but it was easier to concentrate on your voice once I'd stopped talking."

For a moment, they didn't say anything. They huddled in the dark and listened. They heard nothing at first, and then—*footsteps.* Slow . . . pounding . . . footsteps.

They both wanted to run away, but to where? The thumping, echoing footsteps—*tha-rump . . . tha-rump . . . tha-rump*— sounded as if they were coming at them from everywhere at once.

"Bienvenue, mes amis!"

"Jean-Remy!" Elliot cried. "Is that you?"

"Bien sûr! Why do you look so frightened?"

"Wait. How do you know we look frightened?" asked Leslie.

Jean-Remy laughed. "Ze darkness? *Meh,* it is no problem for me! I am a fairy-bat. In ze dark, I can see perfectly well! It is simply in my nature. Well, half of it, you see?"

"We look *scared,*" Elliot explained, "because Grinner is somewhere in here with us."

"Zat bigmouth ghork? No-no-no, do not worry about him. We dropped him off already—in ze Simmersville Lake!"

"But we heard footsteps," said Elliot. "*Big* footsteps."

"But of course! Zat was Gügor."

"Hello," came a deep, dopey voice. "Welcome aboard."

The chamber lurched once again. Elliot and Leslie were thrown to the floor.

"Sorry," said Jean-Remy. "Ze pilot, he is still—how do you say—learning ze ropes. But he is very skillful. Most others, zey would have crashed by now."

"Very reassuring," said Leslie.

"Would somebody mind turning on the lights?" asked Elliot.

"Don't worry," said Gügor. "They'll be here soon."

"*They?*" asked Elliot.

"Ah! Here they come."

A faint bluish-green glow seeped into the darkness above them. Streams of colorful light, fading softly through every color of the rainbow, illuminated the dimly visible ceiling.

"Luster bugs!" cried Leslie. She recalled how, when they had first discovered the Creature Department and were lost in the tunnels below it, the luster bugs had guided them to safety. She would always have a special fondness for these gentle, luminous creatures.

Gügor admired them, too. He gazed upward, his colorful dreadlocks spilling down the back of his neck. "*Beee-yoo*iful," he intoned.

They *were* beautiful, but as the chamber brightened, they saw that it wasn't just luster bugs above them.

"W-*w-where* are we?" asked Elliot.

"The engine room," said Gügor. He smiled proudly and cracked his enormous knuckles.

They were standing at the center of a vast tumult of machinery. Only it wasn't machinery. It looked like the pulsating internal organs of a *living thing*! This was nothing like being in an engine room. This was like being in the rib cage of some incredible beast. Translucent tubes, wide as plumbing pipes, corkscrewed in every direction. They covered the chamber walls and pumped with what could only be described as blood. Above them, veiny white lungs (as big as a pair of buses!) inflated and subsided with a slow, steady rhythm. Between them, a glistening, pulsating heart muscle throbbed and juddered—*ba-doom, ba-doom, ba-doom . . .*

"It was Patti and Harrumphrey who designed ze flying machine," Jean-Remy said, nodding. "Since it is a biomechanical machine, it needs ze biomechanical guts, you see?"

"Makes sense," Leslie admitted, "in an ooey-gooey, creaturely sort of way."

"That's the best way of all," said Gügor.

Surrounded by so many twitching and pulsating biomechanical organs, it was easy to be distracted. Only then did Elliot and Leslie notice Jean-Remy and Gügor were dressed in tuxedos and top hats.

"Where's the party?" asked Elliot.

Jean-Remy looked down at himself. "It is because of your uncle. He insisted on a full dress rehearsal."

"You mean for the cabaret?" asked Leslie.

Jean-Remy nodded sadly. "He made us build an entire stage in ze main cabin, just so we could practice. I really do zink he is taking zis disguise *a little too* seriously."

"Maybe we can talk to him," Elliot suggested.

Jean-Remy nodded. "If you would be so kind. Now, come, we will take you upstairs to meet ze others."

The main cabin of the flying machine didn't look like an airplane at all. It looked more like a grand old concert hall. The seats were of a plush blue velvet, while the walls alternated between the soft sparkle of gold leaf and the gleam of polished wood. Many of the creatures of DENKi-3000 were already on the stage: Harrumphrey, Patti, Reggie, and even the hobmongrels, Bildorf and Pib, every one of them dolled up in top hats and tails.

"Where's my uncle?" Elliot asked Patti, when they entered the cabin.

Patti lowered her voice. "Behind the curtain," she whispered.

"Uncle Archie?" Elliot called.

Professor von Doppler's head popped out from where the curtains met. "*Excellent!* I'm so glad we found you." He raised his eyebrows, and his top hat, which was a bit too big for his head, slipped down over his eyes. He tilted his head back to see under the brim. "We'll be needing an audience. It's crucial you tell us what you think."

"Are you sure now's the time? We're here to rescue Eloise-Yvette, Jean-Remy's sister—remember? We're not *actually* performing in the food festival cabaret."

"Elliot's right," said Leslie. "Just now, we barely escaped from Grinner. The ghorks are planning to do something terrible at the festival, and we don't even know what it is yet!"

"All of that's true," said the professor, "but you're forgetting something."

"We are?"

"Of course! What is it I'm always telling you?"

"There's a little creature in everyone?" Elliot suggested.

"No," said the professor. "The *other* thing I'm always telling you."

Elliot and Leslie looked at each other.

"Oh," said Leslie. "I know."

Elliot knew, too. Ever since they had saved DENKi-3000 with a series of bizarre inventions, Professor von Doppler had said it many, many times.

"There's more than one way to save the day," they recited in unison.

"*Precisely*," said the professor. "When you're dealing with ghorks, you have to be prepared for every eventuality!"

"Even cabaret?" asked Elliot.

"Why not? Without a good disguise, we'll never sneak into Simmersville undetected. And any good disguise is *so much more* than just an unusual outfit. In order to be convincing, we're going to have to *completely inhabit* our roles as traveling cabaret performers. That means practice! In the meantime, why doesn't Reggie introduce you to our pilot? Quite a dashing fellow." With that, the professor's head—top hat and all—vanished behind the curtain.

"The pilot?" asked Leslie.

"Indeed," said Reggie, clomping toward them in his enormous galoshes. "Old Clutchie, a dear old friend of mine! A magnanimous maestro of derring-do! A hero for all seasons! Well, mostly winter—on account of being a fellow Antarctican."

Reggie led them through the crowd of creatures and across the main cabin to a narrow door at the front of the beetle.

"Ahem!" Reggie rapped the door with his blubbery knuckles.

In response, the Coleopter-copter careened sickeningly to one side.

"Apologies," drawled a voice from inside the cockpit. "You broke my concentration."

"Reggie here, old chap. A couple of important visitors would like to see you at work. Would you mind if we came in?"

"It's your funeral."

Reggie chuckled. "Ho-ho! That's Old Clutchie for you. Such a joker!"

Reggie opened the door and they saw that, in contrast with the old theatrical atmosphere of the main cabin, the flying machine's cockpit glowed with modernity. Gauges, switches, buttons, dials, and view-screens covered every surface. Running down the center were so many levers it looked like the cockpit floor was wearing a mohawk, and even these were tipped with blinking lights. The only parts that didn't twinkle with technology were the windows, two darkly tinted domes that peered out into the starry night.

Seated at the center of it all was the pilot, his hands moving lightning quick from lever to lever. With his back turned, it was impossible to see his face. All they saw of him was a pair of antlers, branching out on either side of the bucket seat. Then, in the dark sheen of the cockpit windows, Elliot and Leslie made out the smoky reflection of a face.

"Elliot, Leslie," said Reggie. "Allow me to introduce Cosmo Clutch. 'Old Clutchie' to his friends."

"Old Clutchie" looked like a cross between a yak, a reindeer, and a swashbuckling pirate. He was dressed in a black leather trench coat and goth riding boots, with an eye patch over one eye, a soul patch growing under his lower lip, and a big brown cigar sticking out of his mouth. His hands, sporting only three thick fingers each, gripped tightly to the steering controls.

"Pleased to meet you, Mr. Clutch," said Leslie.

Cosmo Clutch didn't move. His eyes—or rather, the one that wasn't covered with a battered patch—remained fixed on the controls. Elliot and Leslie couldn't help but stare.

"You've never seen a creature like me before, have you?" asked Cosmo Clutch.

"Does that surprise you?" asked Leslie.

Elliot, who was always interested in meeting new creatures, said, "What kind are you, anyway?"

"Guess."

"A hairy yakman?" Elliot tried.

"Nope."

"A fuzzy antlerox?"

"Try again."

"How about *an unhelpful pain in the neck*?" suggested Leslie.

Cosmo smiled. "Getting warmer."

"How are we supposed to *guess*?" asked Leslie. "There must be a million different kinds of creatures in creaturedom!"

"*Actually*," said Harrumphrey, hobbling up to join them by the cockpit, "there aren't nearly that many. I believe the precise number is eleven thousand, five hundred, and twenty-two distinct species."

Leslie blinked at him. "You really are a walking brain, aren't you?"

Harrumphrey nodded proudly. "I may be the only creature in creaturedom who has memorized them all. And if I'm not mistaken, our pilot friend here would belong to creature type one thousand, seven hundred, and seventy-four, subset C."

They all stared blankly at Harrumphrey.

"A snub-snouted danger-moose!"

"Bingo," said the pilot.

"Danger-moose?" asked Elliot.

"Native to the creaturely realms of both the north and south poles," Harrumphrey explained, "but quite rare on account of the fact that so many of them perish in feats of ill-advised daredevilry."

"It's the antlers," Cosmo explained, pointing to the side of his head. "They put pressure on the part of my brain devoted to fear. So I never feel any."

"Which is why he's the perfect pilot for a Coleopter-copter," said Reggie.

"You don't experience fear," said Elliot. "Is that why you're smoking in the cockpit?"

Cosmo Clutch laughed. *"Hah!* Who's smoking?"

"You are." Elliot pointed to the massive cigar in Cosmo's mouth.

"Relax. This baby's *one hundred percent chocolate.* The dark stuff, of course." He plucked it out to show how the tip had melted between his teeth.

"A chocolate cigar?" asked Leslie.

"You got a problem with that?"

"Nope."

Professor von Doppler came up behind Harrumphrey, poking his head into the cockpit. Slung around his neck was a steam-powered keytar, an instrument that was part piano, part banjo, part teakettle.

"Come on, you two," he said. "We're just about to start rehearsal, and we desperately need to hear what you think. If our performance isn't good enough, no one will believe we're really cabaret performers!"

"We're *not* cabaret performers," Harrumphrey harrumphed.

"You are today," the professor told him. "Now come on!"

EAR PLUNGER

CHAPTER 11

In which Reggie discovers a whole new vocal range

The *Creature Book of World Records* lists the Top Three silliest things in creaturedom as follows:

1. A bombastadon's midwinter boot-washing festival.

2. The wardrobe of a Dandimalion schboov.

3. A screaming wee-beast with laryngitis.

However, if the officials from the *Creature Book of World Records* had been present to witness the performance of the DENKi-3000 Creature Department that night, they might very well have crowned a new champion.

Elliot and Leslie were seated alone near the middle of the main cabin. All the other seats were empty because the creatures had assembled behind the curtains at the rear. The professor's voice crackled over the intercom.

"Ladies and gentlemen! Prepare to—no, wait. That's not right, is it? *Lady* and gentle*man*! It is my great pleasure to—hold on. How old do you have to be to qualify as a lady? How old are you two?"

"*We're twelve!*" Elliot shouted back at him. "And we're on a *rescue mission*! We don't have time for a musical number."

"Oh, I've got it!" said the professor. "*Young* lady and *young* gentleman! That's the one! Young lady and young gentleman, prepare to be amazed!"

The lights in the main cabin dimmed. There was an electric whir as every seat turned 180 degrees to face the stage.

"And now," crackled the professor's voice, "bringing you to a whole new level of in-flight entertainment, may we humbly present: The DENKi-3000 Creature Cabaret!"

The curtains parted, and Elliot and Leslie giggled. They couldn't help it. It was funny to see all their creaturely friends, huddled awkwardly together in stiff fancy dress, blinking into a spotlight. The professor walked onstage to join them. *Click-click-clickety-click* went his shoes. Elliot and Leslie realized that the shiny wingtips everyone was wearing were actually *tap-dancing shoes*!

"Seriously," said Elliot. "We don't have time for this." He was about to unbuckle his seat belt and voice another objection, when the music started.

At the rear of the stage, a row of creatures formed the band. They were holding oddly shaped guitars, drums, horns, and flutes. Off to one side of the stage was the professor himself, calibrating his keytar. On the opposite end was Gügor, who held an enormous clockwork horn (it was a homemade electrombone, rickem-ruckemed together from bits and pieces in the Creature Department). Then, all together, they began to play. It sounded like an orchestra featuring nothing but tubas and accordions (and perhaps one or two steam engines), and then . . . *the singing*:

WE ARE CREATURES!
WE ARE LEGION!
WE'RE FROM EVERY CREATURE REGION!
BLOW YOUR TRUMPET!
BANG YOUR DRUM!
MARCH ALONG WITH CREATUREDOM!

Patti stepped forward, with Jean-Remy hovering beside her. With each step, they performed bowlegged dips in time to the music's jaunty beat. Jean-Remy took up the first line:

Excuse me, madam, but what is zat?
Something *slimy* under your hat!

Patti doffed her top hat.

It's no big whoop. Don't be freakin'.
My hair up top? It's *always* leakin'!
Now you, my friend, so pale and pretty
How come you're so itty-bitty?

Jean-Remy responded with a typically Gallic shrug.

My father? He was a vampire-bat.
Ma mère? A fairy. So zat is zat!

Pumping their arms foolishly, they knee-dipped back into the crowd as the chorus struck up again:

WE ARE MISFITS!

> WE ARE CREATURES!
> WE HAVE SPOOKY CREATURE FEATURES!
> HORNS AND FANGS!
> TEETH AND TAILS!
> AND POORLY TENDED FINGERNAILS!

Next, Harrumphrey toddled to the front of the stage, along with Gügor and his electrombrone. Harrumphrey, of course, looked more disgruntled than ever (which was saying a lot). Nevertheless—and *very* reluctantly—he muttered in time to the music:

> Singing? Bah! It's not for me.
> I'm singing this begrudgingly.

He tried returning to the wings, but the others jostled him back to finish his lines.

> I'm Harrumphrey, kinda dumpy.
> Mostly head and mostly grumpy!
> That's okay; I can't complain.
> Underneath . . . I'm mostly brain!

Gügor came forward with two booming steps.

> Gügor is a knucklecrumpler.
> Nothing rhymes with knucklecrumpler.
> What is Gügor's claim to fame?
> It's in the knucklecrumpler name.
> Gügor CRUMPLES! That's because:
> Gügor is as Gügor does.

And so on. . . .

Every time the creatures returned to the chorus, Reggie tried to muscle his way in front of everyone else, doing his best to steal the limelight. It never worked, of course, but his efforts only added to the sense of blundering, ridiculous comedy. Intentional or not, the performance was *hilarious*!

Even though Elliot was worried they really ought to be planning their attack on the Heppleworth Food Factory, he couldn't help giggling. Leslie was cracking up, too. In fact, they were laughing so hard they had to undo their seat belts so they could (literally) roll in the aisles. The DENKi-3000 Creature Cabaret was the funniest thing they had ever seen!

At last, the *oompah-pah* music, the knee bends, the jazz hands, and the ridiculous lyrics all built to a final crescendo. Reggie realized this was his last chance to prove he was the true star of the show. He thundered forward with the ferocity of a bombastadon heading off to war, knocking down all but a single creature. One fuzzy, purple accordionist, bravely played on at the back of the stage.

The rest of the creatures lay in a heap below the footlights, all of them glaring up at Reggie. Misinterpreting their anger as expressions of awe and encouragement, Reggie assumed his moment in the limelight had finally arrived. He clomped down on one knee, spread his arms, and belted out the final line of the song.

And so it goes in
CREEEEEEEE-
CHUUUUUUURRR-
DOOOOOOOOOOOOOOOOOOOOOOOMMMM!

It was that final syllable that did it.

The flying machine quivered as if it had hit a pocket of turbulence. But it wasn't the air *outside* the flying machine that caused everything to tremble; it was the hot air *inside*—Reggie's hot air. The big bombastadon had always had a deep, resonant voice, but when he arrived at the final DOOOOOOMMM in "creaturedom," he discovered a whole new vocal range. Perhaps even a whole new *sound*.

Elliot and Leslie covered their ears. So did everyone else.

"Reggie! *Stop!*" cried the professor. "The show's over!"

But Reggie was oblivious. With his eyes shut tight, his jowls flapping freely around the huge O of his mouth, he held that seemingly bottomless final note.

"Reggie! No!"

But it was too late. The vibration of Reggie's singing was so violent that—

K-K-K-K-K-K-KRRRACK!

The windows began to shatter. They broke in quick succession from the stage all the way to the front of the cabin. When the sound reached the cockpit door, it shattered too, splintering to bits.

Cosmo Clutch's antlers flailed in the pilot's seat. The gauges and readouts were smashed. Smoke rose from the controls. Warning lights blinked in panic and then gave up completely, falling ominously dark. Perhaps it was this dire image that finally got through to Reggie. Or maybe he simply—*finally*—ran out of air. In any case, he stopped singing.

In the ruins of the cockpit, Cosmo Clutch's cool concentration had shattered as effectively as everything else. He whipped his head frantically from side to side, searching the dashboard for anything that still worked. But nothing did. Old Clutchie could only howl over the wind, rushing in through all the broken windows.

"Pusslegut, you numbskull! *We're going to crash!*"

CHAPTER 12

In which Elliot, Leslie, and Cosmo share an embrace

The Coleopter-copter tumbled through the air. The interior of the cabin had become the strangest tableau in history: a whirling Victorian music hall, filled with creatures of all shapes and sizes, each one dressed in top hats and tap-dancing shoes, flailing and floating in zero-gravity panic.

"*YEEE-HAW!*" cried the danger-moose in the cockpit.

"*AAAIIEEEEEGH!*" screamed everyone else.

Every gauge in the cockpit flashed and bleeped and spun. The mohawk of levers flailed like legs of a millipede as Hercules toppled through cloud after cloud. Through the windows, Elliot and Leslie saw brief glimpses of the ground, soaring up to meet them. At one point, Leslie caught sight of an enormous knife slicing toward them out of the night.

"The Heppleworth towers!" she cried.

Then they were swallowed by another cloud.

"Any chance I could I get some help up here?" Cosmo called into the cabin. "Might be a few too many levers for just one danger-moose."

Leslie and Elliot were closest to the cockpit, so they fought against the tipping and flipping of the flying machine to drag themselves forward.

"Glad you could make it," said Cosmo Clutch.

"What can we do?" asked Elliot.

"Group hug," said Cosmo.

"What do you need a hug for?" asked Leslie. "I thought you were fearless."

"Not each other. I mean hugging the levers!" Cosmo was struggling to gather all of them toward him, but there were simply too many. "If we can pull 'em all in, all at once, they'll lock the wings open and set us steady. *I think.* A group hug oughta do it."

Elliot reached for a lever, but it whipped beyond his grasp.

"Not yet," Cosmo instructed. "On my count. Three . . . two . . . one . . . *now!*"

All three of them scooped as many levers as their arms could hold, drawing them together. Coincidentally, pulling all these levers together did indeed result in a group hug, with Elliot, Leslie, and Cosmo all huddled together at the center of the cockpit.

"This is cozy," said Cosmo Clutch.

"Now what?" asked Elliot. He was keen to get away from the pilot, whose furry face smelled a bit too strongly of bitter cocoa. Also, his left antler was poking into his cheek.

"Keep holding on," said Cosmo Clutch. "The forewings haven't locked yet."

It was true: The flying machine was still careening this way and that, and the multitude of levers still twitched against their chests. Then, all at once—*kerrrr-LUNK!*

Every one of the levers locked in place, and the flying machine steadied itself. Back in the main cabin, everyone came down with an unceremonious *whoomp* (and dizzily returned to their seats to fasten their seat belts).

"See? Nothin' to it!" said Cosmo Clutch.

Leslie peered out through the windows, but all she saw were the flying machine's enormous pincers, jutting forward into a dark mist. "Can we please land now?" she asked.

One of Cosmo's furry fingers tapped the dashboard. "Hard to say. Pusslegut's smash-tastic singing voice fried my instruments. Won't even know how high we are till we make it out of this cloud."

As he said this, the fog in front of them took on an eerie green glow that brightened slowly as the mist cleared to reveal: *a wall of glass.*

"AAIIIEEEEGH!"

They were only meters above the ground, skimming over a grassy courtyard. The three cutlery towers loomed above them. They were flying through the grounds of the Heppleworth Food Factory . . . straight for the lobby of the spoon building.

CRASH!

The flying machine's beetle horns ruptured the glass, and they skidded across a huge marble foyer until, at last, the bizarre beetle-shaped machine bumped to a halt.

"Everybody okay back there?" asked Cosmo.

Harrumphrey groaned from where he lay under Gügor's knees. "I feel like I just had a knucklecrumpler tap dancing on my face."

"Sorry," said Gügor. "It wasn't on purpose."

Gügor politely lifted his legs so his friend could wriggle out from under him. He climbed to his feet and peered out the window. "Vitamin supplements," he read off a huge sign, now lying on the marble floor, strewn with shards of broken glass. "Wholesome breakfast cereal. Organic canned goods . . ."

"We're inside the Heppleworth headquarters," said Elliot, emerging from the cockpit.

"We just crashed into the lobby of the gigantic spoon," said Leslie.

"So much for taking them by surprise," said Patti.

"Taking *who* by surprise?" asked Elliot. "There's nobody here."

"Just a lot of elevators," Gügor observed. There were ten in all, lining one entire wall of the lobby. "Twenty . . . nineteen . . . eighteen . . . seventeen . . ."

"What are you doing?" Leslie asked him.

"Counting down," said Gügor. "See?" He pointed to the numbers above each of the elevators. The dials above every one counted down in eerily silent unison.

"Five . . . four . . . ," Gügor counted, "three . . . two . . . one . . ."

DA-DING!

All ten elevator doors opened at once, and out poured ten raging waves of ghorks!

CHAPTER 13

In which Elliot and Leslie demonstrate their inventions, and Cosmo Clutch raises a problem with Wednesdays

Ghorks!"

The horde of hideous creatures swarmed around Hercules. Nose-ghorks sniffed the landing gear. Ear-ghorks listened to its thumping innards. Eye-ghorks blinked in the windows. Hand-ghorks peeled away strips of the Coleopter-copter's metal flesh and fed them to the mouth-ghorks, who chewed the iron and copper as thoughtfully as food critics.

Gügor frowned out the window. "Poor Hercules!"

"Time to see if our disguises work!" said the professor. "I'll tell them we're here to perform in the cabaret." Before anyone could object, the professor stuck his head out the nearest hatch. "Excuse us," he called to the swarm of ghorks, speaking in a stiffly polite voice. "We are but humble dinner-theatre-style cabaret performers, already dressed in our outlandish costumes and eagerly looking forward to the Simmersville Food Festival Final Feast. I fear we may've taken a wrong turn. If you would be so kind as to direct us—"

The ghorks growled at him, and the flying machine was pelted with snot-balls (courtesy of the nose-ghorks).

The professor ducked back inside. "I don't think they're buying it."

Jean-Remy, top hat in hand, whizzed across the cabin to alight on Leslie's shoulder. "I believe Elliot and Leslie can help us in zat department."

"We can?" asked Elliot.

"*Bien sûr!* We took ze liberty of packing your inventions."

"Our anti-ghork devices?" asked Elliot.

"But they aren't finished," said Leslie. "We never even tested them."

Patti pointed out the window. "Now's your chance."

The professor pressed a button, and a section of the seats slid away to reveal a hatch in the floor. Inside were five separate compartments filled with a number of the children's devices.

Elliot and Leslie were amazed. At DENKi-3000 Headquarters, these inventions had hardly progressed further than blueprints and a few rickety prototypes. But here in the compartments, there were ten of each invention, all of them shiny and perfectly built.

"You actually made them!" Elliot cried.

"Precisely to your specifications," said Harrumphrey.

Elliot reached into the first compartment and brought out something that looked like a small crossbow, but in place of the bow it sported a large blue funnel, the narrow end pointing away from the handle. An electric fan was positioned to blow air into the funnel's larger end.

Elliot turned it in his hand, admiring the creatures' handiwork. "This is for the nose-ghorks," he explained. He directed the pointed end of the funnel at Harrumphrey and switched on the fan. A cyclone of air spiraled down the funnel, delivering a fine jet of wind. Harrumphrey's beard rustled.

"No offense," said the hufflehead, "but how's that going to stop a ghork?"

"It's not loaded," said Leslie. "That's what *those* are for." She pointed to the enormous wheels of cheese, sealed in red wax and stored in the same compartment. "Each of those is a wheel of Buffalo Butt Blue cheese. According to Patti, it's the smelliest cheese in the world."

Patti nodded, wrinkling her nose.

Elliot pointed to a small porcelain plate, mounted between the electric fan and the large opening of the funnel. "You put a chunk of Buffalo Butt Blue right here, and fire the smell straight up their noses. We call it the Funky Cheese Wafter."

"Ingenious!" cried Jean-Remy.

Next, the children demonstrated the Onion Stunner, an automated onion-grater device, complete with the world's most pungent onions—for the eye-ghorks, of course. Then there was the Slobber-Robber, a kind of shoulder-mounted cannon designed to lob huge, extra-long-lasting gobstoppers into the jaws of mouth-ghorks. Perhaps the oddest of all was the the Four-Stringed Ear-Stinger, a contraption like a chest-mounted papoose, with a pair of robotic arms sticking out of either side. One robotic claw held a poorly tuned violin, while the other clutched a bow. The arms were programmed to play the instrument like a first-time music student. This, of course, was a tactic to annoy the ear-ghorks into submission. The fifth and final compartment contained wooden catapults that fired extremely soft cushions.

"The rest I understand," said Patti, "but this? Fluffy cushions? What're you gonna do, send 'em to sleep with a bedtime story? Good luck with that."

Reggie came to the children's defense. "Please, do not under-estimate the power of a fluffy cushion! My own regiment made memorable use of bed linen during the berg-biter uprising of 1981. Bombastadon historians refer to our victory as the Million-Pillow Blitz!"

Some of the other creatures groaned (especially Bildorf and Pib). They sensed the blustery arrival of another one of the Colonel-Admiral's long-winded war stories.

Before Reggie could go any further, Elliot agreed with him. "Sometimes the best weapons are the *unexpected* ones." He picked up one of the handheld catapults. It was loaded with a plump pink pillow. "We call this a Fluffy Pillow Pitcher. It's a diversionary tactic." He ran his fingers through the pillow's luxuriant fabric. "With their heightened sense of touch, those hand-ghorks are going to find these irresistible—which'll hope-fully give us time to escape."

"Maybe we should escape *right now*," said Bildorf, still quiv-ering in his tiny tuxedo.

Pib nodded enthusiastically. "Are you sure we can go up against those things with nothing but stinky cheese and fluffy cushions?"

"We have to," Elliot told them. "We *can't* run away." He pointed out the nearest window. "Those ghorks are going to tear their way in here whether we like it or not, and if we don't fight back, who's going to save Eloise-Yvette? We have to find her, not to mention find out what the ghorks are up to!"

"Elliot is right," Jean-Remy said. "My sister and I may have our problems . . . she may be terribly vain and selfish, *buuut* . . . as Leslie says, she is my family. Today we are ze only hope she has."

"*Or*, to put it another way," said the professor, "it's time for us to *save the day*!" He stooped to retrieve a Funky Cheese Wafter from the hatch, raising it bravely above his head. "And if there's anyone here who knows a thing or two about saving the day, it's—"

"*Me*," said Cosmo Clutch. The danger-moose stood at the front of the cabin, legs akimbo, hands on his hips, a fiery glint in his one uncovered eye. "I've saved enough days to fill a calendar!"

Patti whistled in appreciation. "He does look *quite* heroic."

Cosmo winked at Patti. "Not just heroic. *Intrepid*."

Patti swooned (a dollop of mud fell from her hair and dribbled down her dress).

"Lemme tell you," said Cosmo, "if there's one thing I've learned in all my years of day-saving, it's this." He took the chocolate cigar out of his mouth and pointed it at the professor. "There are some days—usually Wednesdays—that can't be saved by fighting. Days like that can only be saved by . . . *hmm*." He tapped the cigar thoughtfully against one of his antlers. "What *was* it again?"

"You see?" said the professor. "Just as I've always said! There's more than one way to—"

He didn't finish the familiar phrase. A band of hand-ghorks broke in. They came straight through the back of the cabin, emerging onstage like villains in a Christmas pantomime. In seconds, they had torn the curtains to shreds. The professor, already armed with a Fluffy Pillow Pitcher, fired a lemon-colored cushion into the midst of the ghorks.

The first of them tried to bat it away, but the moment she touched it, she stopped. She hugged the pillow to her chest, and a look of dimwitted satisfaction melted across her face. Shocked by the sudden pacification of their comrade, the other ghorks

approached her. Their huge cucumber-like fingers reached for
the yellow cushion as if it were a sacred relic. The moment their
fingertips touched it, a fight erupted.

Elliot and Leslie smiled proudly at each other. "It's working!"
Elliot cried. "I can't believe it's working!"

Seeing the hand-ghorks incapacitated by a fight over a fluffy
pillow, everyone's confidence was bolstered. Each of the creatures
from DENKi-3000 armed themselves with one of the strange
weapons. They threw open the flying machine's bay doors and
leapt out, ready for a battle of epic (and very odd) proportions.

CHAPTER 14

In which Bildorf and Pib use the direct approach,
Cosmo Clutch proves he's an excellent multitasker,
and Leslie finds an uncommon carrot

Banzai!" cried Bildorf and Pib.

They had strapped swimming goggles over their eyes and tied tiny polka-dotted handkerchiefs over their faces. They looked like shaggy miniature Wild West banditos! The transformation wasn't to disguise their identities, however. It was to protect them from their own stench. Both hobmongrels were too small to carry one of Elliot and Leslie's anti-ghork devices, so they had gone for a more direct approach. Bildorf had rubbed himself in the extra-stinky cheese, while Pib had soaked her fur in onion juice. They both reeked unbearably, which was perfect when they scaled up the backs of the ghorks and smeared themselves across their hideous faces (which was quite effective).

Gügor, meanwhile, went berserk. He rounded up a small herd of ear-ghorks and crumpled them into an ear-flapping mass. When he was done with them, they looked like an enormous pitted green basketball (with gigantic ears).

"What have you done with Gügor's 1TL?!" he hollered at them.

"Look at these ears," one of them whined back at him. "We can hear you just fine! Quit shouting!"

"Also, what's a 1TL?" cried another.

"*Eloise-Yvette*," Gügor growled. "She's Gügor's One True Love!"

The massive green basketball trembled with laughter. "What a sap!"

Gobstoppers, fluffy cushions, onion slices, and clouds of cheesy stink soared in every direction, all to a soundtrack of excruciatingly off-key music.

"It's working!" cried the professor. He waved a pair of polka-dot cushions over his head. "We're doing it! We're fighting back! We're *saving the day*!"

For once, it seemed the professor was right. All across the lobby, the ghorks were taken by surprise, thanks to Elliot and Leslie's ingenious weapons. Even though they were outnumbered ten to one, the creatures of DENKi-3000 were—astonishingly, *miraculously*—winning.

Cosmo Clutch lived up to his word when it came to saving the day. He had an Onion Stunner in both hands, an Ear-Stinger strapped across his chest, and a Fluffy Pillow Pitcher tied into his antlers. Even with all that extra equipment, he still flipped among the ghorks as nimbly as a gymnast.

Over near the elevators, armed with an Onion Stunner (Leslie) and a Funky Cheese Wafter (Elliot), the two children were able to hold back a pair of ghorks. They had cornered a nose-ghork and an eye-ghork, pinning them to the wall with the unspeakable bouquets of onions and Buffalo Butt Blue cheese.

"Tell us what you've done with the creatures who work here," Leslie demanded.

"Where are you keeping Jean-Remy's sister?" Elliot asked, closing in with his Funky Cheese Wafter.

"The same place we're gonna keep you two," replied the nose-ghork, trying in vain to plug his enormous nostrils.

"That's right," said the eye-ghork, his eyes squeezed tight. "We've turned this whole place into one great big dungeon—and we'll have all of you down there soon enough!"

"Not as long as I've got one of these!" Elliot turned the fan on his Stinky Cheese Wafter to full power.

"It's not going to stop," Leslie added, "until you tell us what you're up to!"

Unfortunately, Elliot's stinky cheese weapon worked a little *too* well. With a scream of disgust, the ghorks slid along the wall and ran around the corner behind the elevators. Sensing victory, Elliot and Leslie chased after them, but when they turned the corner themselves, they hit a dead end.

"How did they do that?" asked Leslie.

Elliot lowered his Wafter. "There's no way out."

At the end of the hall, there was nothing but a three-dimensional mural featuring all kinds of food. It was a bit like the highway billboard that had welcomed them to Simmersville. Sculpted fruits and vegetables, meats and fish, grains and nuts, and loaves of bread popped off the wall in a kind of topographical map of dinnertime.

"Could they be hiding behind that sculpture?" Leslie asked.

They walked up to it, running their fingers over the surface, but it was perfectly solid. Then, suddenly, Leslie let out a yelp.

"*Ew!*" She leapt away from the wall, where she had just been examining a basket of artificial carrots and cucumbers.

"That one there! It's . . . *warm*!" She pointed to a carrot that was smaller than the rest. It didn't extend as far as the others. She leaned in for a closer look and saw that what she had taken for a carrot was something else entirely.

"It's a finger!"

"No," said Elliot. "Not a finger. You found *a knottub*! It's like the ones in the Creature Department. I'll bet it's for calling an expectavator."

"There's one way to find out."

Leslie reached into the veggie basket and grabbed the disturbingly warm and lifelike digit (complete with a jagged fingernail and wiry hair on the back of its knuckle). When she pulled it, a hidden door hissed open beside the mural. Inside, they saw the colorful buttons of an expectavator.

"Hiya-hiya!" came a cheerful voice that seemed to twinkle as brightly as the buttons. "Welcome to Heppleworth Food Factory Expectavator Number One! My name is Sunny, and it is my sincerest *hope* to guide you through the hallowed hallways and secret crevasses of—*well, well*! What a pleasant and unexpected surprise! Such a treat to take a couple of youngsters for a ride! Where to, you two?"

Inside the expectavator was one of the oddest creatures they had ever seen. It looked like a bright orange hairball with hands and a face, which wore an expression of pure, wide-eyed happiness. Instead of two legs, the creature had only one. It spiraled in a circle to the floor of the expectavator like a coiled spring, upon which he was blithely bobbing up and down.

"You are coming in, aren't you?"

Whatever it was, the creature inside the expectavator seemed harmless enough, but Elliot and Leslie couldn't just leave their friends. They turned back toward the main lobby, but the moment they rounded the corner, they saw there was trouble. The creatures of DENKi-3000 had run out of ammunition. The hand-ghorks had fought so fiercely over the fluffy pillows, they had torn them to shreds. With nothing remaining to fight over, they could devote their enormous hands to destroying the other weapons. The creatures of DENKi-3000 had lost their advantage. Already, many of them had been captured, hoisted high in a tangle of nets.

Perhaps the saddest sight of all was Hercules, the incredible flying machine that had brought them here. Its monstrous mechanical body filled one half of the lobby, lying inert on the hard marble floor.

"Don't worry about us," the professor called to his nephew through the net in which he was trapped. "We'll be okay! It's up to you and Leslie now! Find Eloise-Yvette! And find out whatever it is these ghorks are up to!"

"Shut it, four-eyes," said one of the ghorks guarding the professor's net (it was an eye-ghork, of course, who would *never be caught dead* wearing spectacles). He thumped Elliot's uncle on the back of his head, knocking the professor unconscious.

"Uncle Archie!" Elliot wanted to run to his uncle's aid, but it was impossible. There were simply too many ghorks—and they were coming straight for them!

They turned and ran for the expectavator.

"Hiya-hiya!" Sunny bounced on his springy leg and rubbed his hands together. "I'm *so* glad you're back! It's going to be *so* exciting to take both of you on a ride in my very own expectavator!

Now then, as I was just saying: Where to, you two?"

Leslie waved her arms at him. "Anywhere but here! Just shut the doors already!"

"Hurry!" Elliot told him. "The ghorks are coming!"

"Oh, I'm very sorry, but I can't shut the doors until you give me a destination."

"Eloise-Yvette," said Leslie. "We're looking for *Eloise-Yvette Chevalier*. Can you take us to her?"

"Oh, Eloise-Yvette! So lovely, isn't she? But . . ." Sunny's brow wrinkled in thought. "I'm afraid when Quazicom took over, Eloise-Yvette was laid off."

"No," said Elliot. "She wasn't laid off. She was thrown in a dungeon!"

"Dungeon? Oh, well! Why didn't you say so? That's something else that changed when Quazicom took over. They installed a whole lot of new buttons in all the expectavators. See?" He pointed to a section of buttons behind them. They were all marked with the same word: *Dungeon #1, Dungeon #2, Dungeon #3*, all the way up to—well, there were too many to count. "Which one would you like?"

"*Any* of them!" Leslie cried. "We don't care! Just press a button and close the door!"

"Oh, no, I could never do that!" said Sunny. "You're my passengers. *You* have to decide."

The first of the ghorks had rounded the corner, rushing down the hall toward the expectavator.

"We'll start at the beginning," said Elliot. "Dungeon Number One!"

Sunny clapped his hands. "Excellent choice!"

Leslie and Elliot backed away from the doors, watching in terror as a horde of eyes, ears, noses, mouths, and hands came glaring and flapping and snorting and growling and grabbing toward them.

The horrifying image vanished just in time, as the doors slid shut. After that, there was only the quiet hum of the expectavator, beginning its descent, down and down and down, to Dungeon Number One.

CHAPTER 15

In which every expectavator needs the right operator,
and the ghorks need a spelling lesson

"Are you sure you're really an expectavator operator?" asked Leslie. She was staring at Sunny, the small orange spring-loaded creature who had welcomed them aboard. He was bobbing (like a recently popped jack-in-the-box) to the soft bossa nova music that fizzled from a speaker in the ceiling. "I mean, aren't you a little too . . ." Leslie wasn't sure how to put it.

"Chirpy?" Sunny suggested.

"That's it! I thought you had to be depressed to run an expectavator, because they're powered by hope. If the operator's too optimistic, you overload the system. Isn't that right?"

Sunny nodded enthusiastically. "Oh, yes! That's true! But you also have to account for where the expectavator is, and what sort of people—or creatures—are using it on a daily basis. We used to have some *stupendously* gloomy expectavator operators around here, but after Quazicom took over, *everyone* around here was depressed. The expectavators barely got off the ground!"

"But wait," said Leslie. "If everyone was depressed after the takeover, how come you're so happy?"

Sunny responded with a good-natured shrug. "I can't help it. I'm a spring-heeled optimistimonster."

"A spring-heeled optimistimonster," Leslie repeated, slowly sounding out the syllables. "I should have known."

"I get it," said Elliot. "You don't *have to be* depressed to operate an expectavator, you just have to possess a disposition that's inversely proportional to the general mood of the surrounding organization."

Sunny and Leslie stared at Elliot.

"You sound more and more like Harrumphrey every day," Leslie told him.

"Thank you!" said Elliot.

DA-DING!

The expectavator doors slid open on a dark and deserted tunnel.

"I hope you enjoyed your trip," said Sunny. "It was a distinct pleasure serving you this evening, and I do hope we'll be seeing much more of you in the future!" He spread one helpful hand into the murkiness beyond the threshold. "You'll find Dungeon Number One just ahead on the right. Have a nice day!"

With that, Elliot and Leslie stepped into the darkness. The expectavator doors sealed silently shut, leaving no trace of themselves. All that remained was a craggy wall of stone. The tunnel looked much like the ones beneath DENKI-3000: a dusty pathway, rough stone walls, roots and crags poking down from the ceiling. Here and there, glass domes bulged out from the rock, flickering with luster bugs. Neither Elliot nor Leslie was quite sure of what they would find in Dungeon Number One, but what awaited them was a complete surprise.

They saw a faint glow of light, bleeding from a small room,

sealed away behind iron bars. Beside it, hand-painted in a child-ish scrawl, was a signpost that read: **DUNJIN #1**.

The room beyond the iron bars was no bigger than Professor von Doppler's office at DENKi-3000 headquarters. In fact, it looked quite a bit like the professor's office. There was an old wooden desk and an old wooden chair; there were a few cabinets and bookshelves; and along one wall were tables where metal and glass chemistry sets bubbled with colorful fluids.

Sitting at the desk was a squat old man with long gray hair falling past his shoulders. He was dressed in a threadbare brown cardigan with corduroy patches over the elbows. Elliot thought there was something familiar about that cardigan. . . .

"*Sir William?* Is that you?"

Slowly, the man at the desk turned around, and they saw that it *certainly wasn't* Sir William Sniffledon, the CEO of DENKi-3000. In fact, the figure wasn't even a human being. *It was a creature.* His long gray hair disguised a broad mustard-yellow face that somewhat resembled that of a toad. He had large, sad, glistening eyes and a wide slit of a mouth, stretching all the way across his face.

"This is a surprise," he croaked. "Who might you be?"

Elliot grasped the cold iron bars. "My name's Elliot and this is Leslie, and we came here with the creatures of DENKi-3000. We're sort of on a rescue mission, except we haven't got to the rescuing part yet."

"More like the opposite," said Leslie. "Now the rescue party needs rescuing!"

Elliot and Leslie explained the letter they had received from Eloise-Yvette and how their friends had been captured after crashing into the Heppleworth lobby.

"Well," said the creature. "I certainly hope you succeed in your mission. As you can see, I could use a little rescuing myself."

"How long have you been down here?" Leslie asked him.

The creature looked down at his soft amphibious fingers, counting them off one by one. It was impossible to tell if he was counting weeks, months, or years. "Too long," he said at last.

"Don't worry," said Elliot. "We're going to find a way to free everyone and return this company to its rightful owners."

The creature's eyes widened. "Are you now?"

Elliot nodded emphatically (though he had no idea how they would accomplish this).

"In that case," said the creature in his tiny cell, "let me thank you in advance . . . for giving it back to me."

"*To you?*" asked Leslie.

"Who else?" The small, toad-like creature rose to his feet and gave them a curt bow. "My name is Dr. Benedict Heppleworth, and this is my company."

CHAPTER 16

In which the chief's secret (and very evil) plan is revealed, but no one believes it

Y ou run your company from an underground dungeon?" Elliot asked.

Dr. Heppleworth shook his broad, creaturely head. His mouth curled into a sad smile. "It was the great success of my products that attracted the attention of the Chief and his ghorks. One product in particular brought them here. Something I called Knoo-Yoo-Juice."

Leslie nodded. "We know all about that stuff. It's an elixir that disguises creatures as people."

Heppleworth nodded. "There will always be creatures who wish to . . . how shall I put it? *Cross over*, I suppose. Knowing this, I began experimenting, and the result was Knoo-Yoo-Juice."

"Is that why the ghorks took over?" asked Elliot. "They want to disguise themselves as people?"

Heppleworth shook his head. "No. I'm afraid it's something much worse. What the ghorks want is quite the opposite."

It took a moment for Heppleworth's words to sink in, but when the old creature's meaning took shape in their minds, Leslie and Elliot looked at each other in horror.

"Oh, no," said Leslie. "You mean . . ."

Elliot gasped. "They want to *turn people into ghorks!*"

"That's right," Heppleworth croaked. "You see, ghorks aren't the cleverest of creatures. More than anything else, they lack creativity. I believe this may be an unintended result of spending so many generations breeding themselves to augment a single sense. Creativity, you see, has much in common with food and drink. Like any great meal, it requires *all* the senses working in concert. The ghorks, however, each obsessed with only one sense at a time, have lost all vestiges of inspiration and inventiveness."

"I guess that makes sense," said Elliot, even though he was reluctant to admit that inventiveness had much in common with appreciating food, which was basically what his parents did for a living.

"Those ghorks," Heppleworth went on, "can see no better way of improving something apart from making it bigger. More beautiful? More subtle? More complex? *More interesting?* All these measures are meaningless to ghorks! Now I'm afraid they plan to apply this same idea to their armies. They intend to start here, in Simmersville, at the food festival."

"But how will taking over the food festival help make their army bigger?"

"Simple," said Heppleworth, "by turning everyone at the festival into a ghork soldier."

"*When?*" asked Leslie. She was thinking of her mother, who would be right at the center of everything.

"Their plan is to do it tomorrow, when everyone is gathered together for the Costume Cabaret. They'll put the elixir into the Final Feast, which is traditionally served following the cabaret."

Heppleworth shut his eyes. "My only hope is they won't discover the formula in time."

"You mean they don't have the elixir?" asked Leslie. "One that'll turn people into ghorks?"

Heppleworth shook his head. "Not yet, but they're very close. Already they've been testing their formulas on the townsfolk, secretly slipping it into dishes at some local restaurant. A place called . . . The Smiling Mudsucker."

Leslie and Elliot looked at each other.

"Oh, no," said Leslie. "We had dinner there tonight!"

"I had *The Special*," said Elliot.

Heppleworth approached the iron bars of his cell. "Turn around," he said. "Let me have a good look at you."

Elliot and Leslie each spun in a circle.

"No horns, no tails, no wings, no claws, no unwanted hair." Heppleworth sighed in relief. "So far, so good."

"What about that girl we saw?" said Leslie. "Emily, the clerk at the hotel. There was something wrong with her arm. It was all green and scaly. It must have happened because she drank one of the ghorks' experimental formulas." She looked to Heppleworth. "But it didn't look like she was turning into a ghork at all. That skin we saw on her arm—it looked like something else. Like a snake or a lizard."

Dr. Heppleworth nodded wearily. "That's the problem. There are just so many different kinds of creatures in the world. Ghorks are only one. So far, they've produced elixirs that turn people into one sort of creature or another, but not yet ghorks— thank goodness!" He stroked his leathery, mustard-colored chin. "The scaly green skin of a snake, you say? Yes, definitely not a ghork, but *oh*! That poor girl!"

"I wish we could help her," said Elliot.

"You *must*," said Heppleworth, grasping the bars with long yellow fingers. "Because it gets worse."

"How could it get any worse?"

"I don't know the details, but there is another reason the ghorks want to increase their numbers. It has something to do with a prophecy. I've heard my guards talking about it, something about a new leader. They've brought him here to Simmersville, and they believe he will guide them to a great victory."

"So it is true," Leslie whispered.

"The Sixth Ghork," said Elliot.

Heppleworth's already bulging eyes widened even further. "A sixth ghork? I've never heard of such a thing."

"*Nobody* has," said Leslie. "But if they brought him to the festival, then maybe—"

Leslie stopped. The sound of marching feet came down the tunnel. Ghorks were coming!

"Hurry!" Heppleworth whispered through the bars. "As of this moment, we three are the only ones who know what Quazicom and the ghorks are really up to. With me locked in here, you two are the only ones who can stop them!" He pointed farther down the tunnel that had brought them here. "Keep going that way. At every fork, turn left. That should lead you back to the market square."

"We can't just leave you in here," said Elliot.

Heppleworth shrugged. "I've already been in here a long time. One more day won't hurt. But please, hurry! They're almost here!"

Reluctantly, they backed away from **DUNJIN #1** and scurried into the shadows, just as the ghorks came pounding around the corner. Elliot and Leslie ran and ran, taking the left side every time the tunnel split.

Eventually, they saw crisscrosses of yellow lamplight, shining down through drainage grates above. At last, they reached a rusty ladder that led up to a grate they could push open. They emerged into an alleyway similar to the one where they had hidden from Grinner. At the end of the alley, they heard the babble and buzz of the Simmersville market square, just as Heppleworth had promised.

"*Leslie Fang!* Where have you been?!" Leslie's mother came rushing across the square. "We've been looking *all over town* for you two!"

Elliot's mother followed close behind. She grabbed her son tightly by his arm. "We've been worried sick," she told Elliot in her sternest voice. "Perhaps you'd like to explain where you've been all this time!"

"You *know* where we've been," Elliot protested. "We've been running away from ghorks all night long!"

His father frowned in disbelief. "You don't expect us to believe that, do you?"

"You were there! You saw him! Grinner even tied you guys up in a tablecloth!"

"Please, Elliot," said his mother. "We've had quite enough of your creature stories."

"Your mother's right," said his father. "That incident in the hotel was nothing more than an eccentric chef in a very good costume. After you two ran off, the waiter apologized—*profusely.*" He shook his head, obviously recalling the fuss. "You know how these genius chefs are. *Temperamental!*"

Elliot waved his arms around the square, indicating the

crowd of festivalgoers. "You guys are as bad as everyone else! Why won't anyone believe us?"

"Because," said his mother, "you are *quite clearly* making all of this up."

"So that's it!" said Leslie's mother. She pulled her daughter until they were face to face. "I just *knew* it!" She waved a finger at Elliot. "You little Lothario! I'll bet you dragged Leslie off for more of your sneaky *smooching*!"

"What?! No!" Leslie fought free of her mother's grip. "And what do you mean—*more*? We've never smooched, not even once! Everything Elliot said is true!"

"Please," Elliot told his parents. "You have to believe me! I know you think they're weird, and yes, they're all creatures, but they're still my friends, and they're in trouble!"

"Friends?" asked his mother. "What about Leslie? Isn't she your friend?"

"Not if they've been smooching, she isn't," said Leslie's mother.

"*Mom!* Enough with the smooching! Elliot's right, and those creatures are my friends, too."

Elliot's father crouched down until he and Elliot were face-to-face. "You may not like to hear this," he said, "but listen, son. Have you and Leslie ever considered finding some new friends?"

Elliot's mother nodded. "Maybe some that aren't so . . . creaturely."

When he heard this, Elliot felt sick. It wasn't simply that his parents didn't believe his friends were in trouble. It was that they didn't believe he should even be friends with them in the first place. He wondered if what he had told Leslie in the darkness of the Coleopter-copter might really be true. Maybe he and his parents were just too different to understand one other.

As his parents dragged him back to the hotel, Elliot was convinced he and his parents might truly be of a different species. *If that's true,* he thought, *maybe I don't belong with them at all. Maybe I belong . . . in creaturedom.*

CHAPTER 17

In which Digits tries not to lose count, and Reggie makes the fine distinction between "abominable" and "iniquitous"

For the creatures of DENKi-3000, it was a long walk to their dungeon. They were shackled together in a chain gang, shuffling through the shadows and dust. Gügor, Patti, Harrumphrey, Reggie, and all the rest were being marched down a winding tunnel, flanked on every side by an army of ghorks. The only creature missing was Jean-Remy, who had expertly escaped capture.

Leading the way were the Five Ghorks—Grinner, Iris, Adenoid Jack, Wingnut, and Digits—the leaders of the five Ghorkolian tribes. None of them spoke, apart from Digits, who finger-counted the doors of cell after cell after cell . . .

"33 . . . 34 . . . 35 . . ."

Every one of them was empty.

"What's he up to?" Patti whispered, pointing to the vacant dungeons. "If they wanna lock us up, why don't they just go ahead and use one of these?"

"We're not allowed," said Wingnut, whose radar-like ears had picked up the bog nymph's question. "It's because of the Chief, see? When it comes to dungeons, he's got what you might call a favorite number."

"Which one?" asked Gügor.

Iris shrugged. "He calls it *the saddest number in the entire universe*! That's what makes it the perfect number for a dungeon."

"You didn't answer his question," said Harrumphrey. "Which number is it?"

"*Ssh!*" said Iris. "You'll make him lose count."

"48 . . . 49 . . . 50 . . ." counted Digits, starting once again on the long thumb of his first hand. "51 . . . 52 . . ."

"Typical hand ghork," muttered Cosmo Clutch. "Gotta use all his concentration—and *all his fingers*—just to count to ten."

"You'd think with a name like Digits," said the professor, "he might try learning some advanced mathematics."

"66 . . . 67 . . . 68 . . ."

"Look here," said Reggie, chains rattling against the gold and jewels of his ceremonial saber. "You have no right to treat us so appallingly. Do you have any idea who I am?"

"Yeah," said Bildorf, who was perched with Pib on the bombastadon's left epaulette. "He once brought peas to his aunt Agatha!"

"I think you mean *peace to Antarctica*," Pib corrected.

"And I said *CAN IT!*" screeched Iris.

The creatures fell silent, but it wasn't because Iris had shouted at them. Just as Digits counted his way through the eighties ("80 . . . 81 . . . 82 . . ."), they heard something. It was something so beautiful they wanted nothing more than to stop and listen.

What they heard was music. The unseen singer's voice was so pure and bright and crystal clear it seemed to wash away the shadows. Only Gügor recognized it. He even knew the words. That was because a long time ago, in his knucklecrumpler youth, he had played that same melody on creaturedom's first ever elec-trombone.

It was Eloise-Yvette . . . and she was singing their song:

> After sunset, strolling home
> Empty streets, I'm all alone.
> The sky is deep and full of stars
> There's nothing like this feeling.

> Beneath a city no one sees
> Shadows feel like friends to me.
> The earth is deep and full of life
> My heart could do with healing.

"98 . . . 99 . . . 100 . . . and *finally*," Digits puffed. "Here we are!"

The entranceway was a huge section cut from the wall. This great hole was barred with a spiderweb mesh of iron bars. Above them, carved into an ornate wooden plaque, was a number. The middle zero was lower than its neighboring numerals, so it looked like this:

$$1 \ 1$$
$$0$$

Grinner smiled up at it. "The Chief's right," he said. "That's gotta be the saddest number ever. Looks like some poor old sad-sack, wailing his eyes out!"

The creatures couldn't help but shiver. The number 101 really did look like a crying face, its eyes scrunched tight with tears streaming down.

The professor didn't think it was fair to accuse this particu-lar number of being the saddest in the entire universe. As a man of science, he knew it was just a number. But in light of where they were, even he couldn't stop a chill running up his spine.

"You mean you dug out *a hundred* empty dungeons," he said, "just so you could lock us up in Dungeon 101?!"

"Cool, huh?" said Digits. "It was the Chief's idea."

He unlocked the door and the creatures, freed of their shackles, were pushed inside. Dungeon 101 was as vast as the Creature Department laboratory at DENKi-3000, and surprisingly, just like the laboratory, it was full of computer mainframes, strange apparatuses, and jumbled heaps of arcane equipment. It was also full of other things: comically enormous cooking equipment, cauldrons as large as moving vans, cake mixers that towered like cranes, blenders as big as upturned cement trucks.

There were creatures, as well: ankle snypes and mini-gryffs, triple-bearded oven trolls and jellyboned wimplebeests, pit lizards and slobberwolves, and many others that defied description. These were the creatures of the Heppleworth Food factory's own Creature Department. They were gathered in groups around tables covered with pots and pans, bubbling chemicals, and colorful ingredients. Only at that moment, they weren't cooking. They had left their stew pots and chemistry sets to stare up at the fairy-bat floating above them.

It was her. Eloise-Yvette. Gügor's One True Love.

Seeing her again after so many years, the knucklecrumpler gasped. She had the same fine features as Jean-Remy, but there was a softness to the curves of her heart-shaped face, her plump lips, and her mop of black curls (kept in check by a braided tassel, tied around her pale blue forehead).

"That's enough!" Grinner sneered, clanking open the gates. "Knock it off and get back to work!"

"*Googy!*" cried Eloise-Yvette, when she saw her old friend. She soared straight for him and wrapped her arms around his neck.

Gügor's whole body tingled. He knew he was blushing, but he couldn't help it. The rosiness began in his toes and bloomed upward, turning him peachy-pink all the way to his colorful dreadlocks.

Eloise-Yvette fluttered up in front of him. "You came to save me! Oh, Googy! *Mmmmwah! Mwah! Mwah! Mwah!*" She pecked four kisses on his cheeks in traditional Parisian style. (Gügor glowed even redder than before.)

Eloise-Yvette hadn't changed at all. Her voice still had the same smoky lilt he remembered, tinged with only the slightest French accent.

"I was worried I might never see you again!"

"Worried?" asked Gügor. A great rabble of butterflies flapped and flipped in his tummy. "You were worried about Gügor?"

"Of course I was worried! I think of you and Jean-Remy as my two brothers. My *blood* brother and my *big* brother!" She giggled and looked past Gügor toward the others. "But where is he?"

The butterflies stopped flipping and flapping. "Brothers," he said, with a note of sadness.

"Of course! But seriously, Googy, where is he? Where's Jean-Remy?"

"Gügor doesn't know. He must have escaped."

Eloise-Yvette sighed. "I have something I wanted to tell him. It is important."

Harrumphrey waddled over, grimacing at Gügor. "Did she just call you *Googy?*"

Gügor didn't answer, but the fact that he went right back to blushing was all the confirmation Harrumphrey needed.

Eloise-Yvette introduced some of her friends from the Heppleworth Food Factory's Creature Department. She explained that this dungeon had previously been the department itself, but when Quazicom took over, it became Dungeon 101, and everyone was locked inside. Now the ghorks were forcing them to concoct an elixir that would do the unthinkable—turn a human being into a ghork.

"*Abominable!*" cried Reggie. "Absolutely abominable! No, hold on a moment. It's *worse* than abominable! It's . . . it's . . . *iniquitous!*" He paused to catch his breath. "Wait, which is worse? Abominable or iniquitous? Oh, dear. I haven't thought this through, have I?"

"You're surprised?" asked Bildorf.

"You never think *anything* through," said Pib.

Eloise-Yvette swooped off to join her friends from the Heppleworth Food Factory Creature Department. All the while Gügor could hardly take his eyes off her.

"So you gonna tell 'er, or what?" asked Patti, reaching up to nudge Gügor in the ribs.

"Gügor is shy," said Gügor, twisting his face.

"You have a supreme grasp of the obvious, doncha, big guy?"

"With hands like those," said Harrumphrey, "he'd have a supreme grasp of *anything*."

Gügor nodded. "That's why Gügor prefers machines. Gügor . . . *understands* them. Besides, wrestling with refrigerators helps Gügor relax."

"Sure," said Patti, "but can you *fall in love* with a refrigerator?"

Gügor had nothing to say to that.

Patti smiled and stroked an encouraging circle around the small of Gügor's back. "You're going to have to tell her how you feel sooner or later."

"Here's how you do it!" Cosmo Clutch stepped up to Gügor, pointing his chocolate cigar in the knucklecrumpler's face. "Like this." He took Patti in his arms as if he were about to stride into a tango.

Patti regarded him suspiciously. "Watch it, bub. One whip of my hair and you'll get a mouthful of swamp."

Cosmo winked at her. "Bit of silt never hurt anybody." To prove it, Cosmo spun Patti in a circle and sent dollops of her bog-nymph clay flying everywhere (even, just as Patti promised, into his mouth). He didn't seem to mind, however, as he cradled her into a low dip, smiled with muddy teeth, and said, "You are, and always will be, the only girl for me!"

Patti giggled.

"See?" Cosmo said, looking up at Gügor. "Nothin' to it."

Cosmo's wooing demonstration was cut short by a huge view-screen looming above them. It flashed and crackled to life, and a shadowy figure appeared. It was the Chief of Quazicom!

His eyes moved over his prisoners, finally settling on Professor von Doppler. "Welcome," he said in his loose, gravelly voice, "to our newest . . . employees."

"We don't work for you," the professor told him defiantly, "and we never will."

"We'll see about that, but first I'd like to thank you for accepting my invitation. I'm so glad you could make it."

The professor folded his arms across his chest. "Invitation? What are you talking about?"

"You know, Professor, for a learned man, you really haven't

learned anything. I'm the Chief; I *always* have a plan. Why else would I let Eloise-Yvette send her little letter? I wanted you here all along, and now here you are, my two favorite Creature Departments in one place." He rubbed his hands together excitedly. "The Heppleworth Food Factory Creature Department will produce my elixir, and the DENKi-3000 Creature Department will produce . . . *my weapons.*"

"We'll do no such thing," said the professor. "If you want a weapon, get your flunkies at Quazicom to make it themselves."

"Quazicom? Produce an actual product?" The Chief laughed like this was the funniest thing he had ever heard.

"You can't, can you?" said the professor. "Because your company—if you can really call it one—has nothing to it. It doesn't *produce* anything! It's an empty shell! A greedy husk of nothingness!"

The Chief nodded smugly. There was something menacing in the way he accepted the worst insults as compliments, as if his whole outlook on life was twisted inside out. "Of course we don't produce anything," he said at last. "You've hit upon the great beauty of the modern global corporation. We no longer need to *produce things*, we merely need to *own* them." He smiled wickedly. "And now I own you."

"You might have locked us up in your dungeon, but you don't own us, and you never will."

"I understand how you might feel that way," said the Chief. "But before you say any more, let me introduce you to Quazicom's unique Incentivization Program."

The professor winced. "Incentivi—is that even a word?"

"It's how we at Quazicom motivate our prisoners—I mean, *employees,*" said the Chief. "After all, motivation is what separates a good employee from a *great* one. Let me show you what I mean."

He snapped his fingers, and the ghorks guarding the dungeon threw open the gates. They poured inside with their clubs and nets and headed straight for Eloise-Yvette.

"*NO!*" cried Gügor. One of the hand-ghorks jumped up to snatch Eloise-Yvette out of the air and when he saw that, Gügor went berserk.

In his mind, he saw every rock, every tree stump, every refrigerator, every vending machine, every bizarre Creature Department invention he had ever punched, kicked, wrestled, crumpled, throttled, or thrashed. Now he did the same to the ghorks, tossing them left and right like old fridges. When the others moved to help him, however, barred walls dropped from the ceiling, corralling them off in one corner. Gügor fought bravely on alone, but it wasn't enough. There were simply too many ghorks for just one knucklecrumpler, no matter how big and strong he was.

"Eloise . . . Yvette," he rasped, as he finally crumpled himself, underneath a pile of fifty ghorks.

Jean-Remy's sister had been taken outside and locked in an enormous cage. It was set on creaking wheels that screeched as a team of ghorks rolled it forward.

"Googy!" Eloise-Yvette called as she was locked inside.

Gügor was so exhausted he couldn't answer. He didn't resist as they dragged his limp body out of the dungeon and threw him in the cage with his 1TL.

"Now then, as I was saying," said the Chief. "This is how Quazicom's Official Incentivization Program works." He looked to the creatures of the Heppleworth Food Factory. "Either you give me an elixir to turn everyone at the food festival into ghorks or I'll grind up your pretty little fairy-bat friend and feed her to my henchmen. And since pretty little fairy-bats don't have much meat on their bones . . ." He turned to the creatures of DENKi-3000. "Either you guys give me a prototype of a shiny new weapon, or I'll grind up the knucklecrumpler, too. *Got it?*"

Every one was stunned into silence.

"I'll take that as a yes," said the Chief. "You have until tomorrow evening, at the Costume Cabaret."

TOOTHLESS COMB

CHAPTER 18

In which Elliot tells his parents what he really thinks,
and Jean-Remy starts a rumor

The next morning, Elliot awoke to the sound of his
mother and father in the bathroom, getting ready
for the day. It was Saturday, the day of the Costume
Cabaret, and he lay alone in bed, feeling groggy and disori-
ented. After his parents had dragged him back to the hotel,
he had hardly slept. He was too worried about his friends. In
fact, he worried so much he had made himself sick. Before
finally falling asleep, his head had throbbed, his stomach had
churned, even his fingers and toes had tingled, especially the
fingers of his right hand. . . .

Now, lying in bed the following morning, he was surprised
to feel a faint prickling in those same fingertips. He couldn't help
but bring his right hand up to his face and—

"AAIIIEEEEGH!"

"Elliot! What is it?" His parents came rushing out of the
bathroom.

Before they could see his hand, he whipped it back under the
covers. "I-I'm fine," Elliot assured them (although this was *definitely* not true). "I was just having a nightmare."

His mother sat down on the edge of the bed and peeled a few locks of hair off Elliot's forehead. "What was it about?"

Beneath the covers, Elliot used his left hand to explore his right. He felt . . .

Hair!

It started at his wrist and went bristling all the way down to his fingertips—which were topped off with what felt like *curving claws*. Something was very, very, *very* wrong with his hand, and he was just about to show his parents when his father said, "Nightmare, huh? Maybe that's what happens when you hang out with Archie and his 'creatures' all the time."

Elliot's mother giggled. "Oh, Peter! You're such a bully sometimes!"

Elliot's frustration from the night before returned to him. Whatever was wrong with his hand, his parents didn't *deserve* to see it. They wouldn't understand. They would only panic. Even worse, they would probably try to take him to the hospital. When he thought of what Dr. Heppleworth had told him about testing potions on customers at The Smiling Mudsucker, he knew that medicine wouldn't help him. This was a creature problem, and only creatures could help him. He didn't need a doctor; he needed Uncle Archie and his friends.

"I'm fine," he told his parents. "It was just a bad dream. I'd better get dressed. Could you pass me my yellow rugby shirt? It's in my bag." His yellow rugby shirt was a little too big for him. *Specifically*, the sleeves were a bit too long.

"Here you go," said his father, lumping the shirt on the top of the covers. "Hurry up. We don't want to be late for our breakfast reservation."

Elliot pulled the shirt on under the blankets. When he finally emerged, the long sleeves hung (thankfully) well past his finger-tips. As always, he topped off the oversized shirt with his bright green fishing vest.

"You sure it isn't too hot for all that?" asked his father, point-ing to Elliot's layers of clothing.

"Don't tease him, dear," said Elliot's mother. "That's *the style*. You know how kids are these days. It's all baggy this and saggy that. Sleeves must be the new thing."

Elliot nodded emphatically. "There's a kid at my school, his sleeves go all the way to the floor! Everyone thinks he's *super* cool."

Outside, the perimeter of the market square was lined with food stalls. Huge banners shouted:

Welcome to Simmersville! Tonight only!
The Simmersville food festival's all-singing, all-dancing
dinner-theatre-style costume cabaret!

As they neared the other side of the square, Elliot spotted Leslie and her mother. They were behind the dim-sum stall, busily handing out cardboard cups of dumplings.

"Can we go say hi?" Elliot asked his parents, but they pulled him past without stopping.

"We'll come back later," said his mother. "The best time for the stalls is just before the cabaret."

Elliot realized his parents were perfectly willing to spend the entire day sampling food at local restaurants. For him, that was impossible. He had to find Uncle Archie and the creatures.

"Where are we going?" he asked.

"Right here," said his father.

They had come across the market square and entered one of the alleys. Restaurants lined both sides, but where Elliot's father pointed there was only a hazy gap. There was something there, but as much as Elliot stared, all he saw was an indistinct smudge.

"Right *where*?" he asked.

Elliot's father smiled at his wife. "I told you he was going to love it."

"Love *what* ?"

"Look closer," said Elliot's mother. "It helps if you squint a little."

Elliot narrowed his eyes and cocked his head to one side. He saw something: a restaurant. Just barely. He felt like he was looking at it through pebbled glass, or through the wind and rain of a terrible storm. There was the vague shape of an awning and an entrance, with squiggles of indecipherable green writing above it. Then he understood.

"This whole restaurant—it's been blurrified!"

"That's right," said his father. "It certainly didn't look like this last year."

"So you see," his mother continued, "this particular restaurant owes quite a lot to that mad uncle of yours. You, too, I suppose." She gave Elliot a little squeeze.

"It's called The Green Fairy," his father explained. "Everything about it is inspired by the Impressionist period of French painting."

Elliot's mother clapped her hands. "It's like eating haute cuisine *inside an actual* Monet or Renoir!"

Elliot didn't share his parents' enthusiasm for the restaurant itself, but he did feel an unexpected swell of pride. When he and Leslie had helped the creatures invent the device that became the

Impressionisticator™, they had been aiming for an invisibility machine. It was nice to see the device being put to good use.

They stepped inside, and it took Elliot's eyes a moment to adjust. There was something beautiful, even breathtaking, in the way the restaurant seemed to be painted from the bright pastel colors and wobbly brushstrokes of an Impressionist painting. When the maître d' seated them at their table, Elliot was relieved to see the menus hadn't been blurrified. Then again, as soon as Elliot began reading the (perfectly legible) menu, he realized that its clarity wasn't the issue. The problem was that everything was in French.

"Where's Jean-Remy when you need him?" he whispered to himself.

Unable to read the menu, Elliot's eyes wandered the room. He noticed there was one corner that was still in the process of being blurrified.

Over near the patio, the maître d' held a bright orange Impressionisticator™, which looked a bit like an alien ray gun, except instead of a hole going down the barrel, it featured a faintly glowing, half-asleep eyeball peering out from the end. When the man pulled the trigger, the Impressionisticator™ played a lullaby, and the eyeball began to close. As it did, he waved the device over the corner of the room. Slowly, that part of the restaurant became blurrier and blurrier.

"Complimentary hors d'oeuvres," said their waiter. He had arrived at the table with glasses of water and a cheese plate.

"Is that *mimolette*?" asked Elliot's mother, pointing to something that looked like a fossilized cantaloupe, like a softball covered in very unappetizing sawdust.

Elliot's father rubbed his hands together. "Rare stuff!"

The waiter departed, and Elliot's mother picked up the oddly shaped knife lying beside the cheese. "Now then," she said, "why don't we start by teaching you how to use a cheese knife?"

When Elliot reached for it, his mother pulled away, making a little tutting noise. "Elliot, *please*. Roll up your sleeves."

Elliot froze. "But you said it was 'the style,' remember?"

"Perhaps out in the street when you're playing with your friends, but not here." She leaned forward and lowered her voice. "This is *The Green Fairy*."

Elliot whipped both hands under the table. "Can I go to the washroom?"

"No! They just brought us mimolette!"

"But I don't want any mimolette."

"Elliot, how can you say that?"

"It's not like we ordered it. It's complimentary."

"Son," said his father. "You ought to know that a boy's first slice of mimolette is a rite of passage. Being able to speak intelligently about fermented milk products is one of the most important parts of growing up! Now, I want you to put your hands back on the table, roll up your sleeves, and eat this fancy cheese like a man."

Elliot couldn't do it. Under the table, his hands (or rather, his hand and *his claw*) were balled up in angry fists. "*No*," he said. "I don't want to talk about food. Or discuss it, or critique it, or analyze it, or anything else that isn't *eating it*!" Elliot couldn't help pounding his fist (the normal one) on the table. "I hope you know that if this was creaturedom, you guys wouldn't even exist! Because they don't have critics in creaturedom. They think it's rude to criticize someone else's hard work, especially when you can't even do that thing yourself, and I think we all know— *you guys can't even cook*!"

Elliot's parents were stunned. His father's jaw hung slack.

His mother's lower lip quivered slightly, and she looked nervously around the restaurant.

"Like I said, I need to go to the bathroom!" Elliot stormed off, the cuffs of his rugby shirt wrapped tightly around his fists. He had never shouted at his parents that way before. As he stalked around the corner toward the toilets, he wondered if his anger had something to do with his hand. Maybe he had changed on the inside, too. Or maybe that was just wishful thinking, an excuse for telling his parents that in creaturedom . . . they wouldn't exist.

As soon as he was alone in the bathroom, Elliot rolled up his sleeve. He almost screamed when he looked at his hand. Thick, moss-green hair had already spread all the way up to his elbow! Yellow-green claws, like the talons of an owl, poked out from his unnaturally long fingers.

What was he going to do?

"You know," said a voice behind him, "you should really have someone examine zat arm."

"Jean-Remy!"

He spun around, and there was the fairy-bat himself, perched atop one of the toilet stalls.

"I must admit," he said, looking around the Impressionistic washroom, "zere is something about zis restaurant zat reminds me of my home."

Elliot was too curious to discuss the decor. "I thought you were captured. What happened?"

"I escaped, ze same as you, in one of ze expectavators."

"But what about the others?" Elliot asked.

"I fear zey have all been captured. You, me, and Leslie, we are ze only ones who can rescue zem."

"Leslie. We'll have to go find her."

"Zere is no need! I've already collected her."

Jean-Remy pointed out through the bathroom's tiny window. Leslie stood outside, holding a steaming cup of dumplings.

"Great," said Elliot, "but if we're going back to Heppleworth's, we can't let anyone see us. I have an idea of how we can sneak back, but we'll need a diversion."

Jean-Remy smiled. "Leave zat to me. . . ."

If you were there that morning, in Simmersville's hazy French restaurant called The Green Fairy, you would have witnessed something very odd. First, you certainly would have noticed the unusual, out-of-focus decor. You might have also noticed a handsome couple in a booth near the wall, sitting at a table with three chairs (one of them empty), hungrily eyeing a cheese plate.

And then . . .

Soaring out of the bathroom came a tiny man with beautiful pearlescent wings, dressed in a disheveled tuxedo. He zipped from one waiter to the next, tipping trays of plates and glasses of wine so they crashed and clattered on the floor. In no time, the whole restaurant was in chaos. (In fact, following this extraordinary incident, a persistent rumor developed that the restaurant was truly haunted by an *actual green fairy*.)

Yes, if you were there that morning, you would have probably been caught up in the chaos. Like everyone else, you probably would have missed the young boy in an oversized yellow rugby shirt, crawling along the back wall to a table, where he picked up something that looked like a science-fiction ray gun with a glowing eyeball on the end. He shoved this strange implement into one of the many pockets in his green fishing vest and crawled away through the patio doors.

CHAPTER 19

In which Leslie becomes a gray haze, Jean-Remy muses on the secret of invisibility, and Elliot isn't quite himself

What happened to your hand?!"

"I think it was something I ate," Elliot told Leslie.

They were in the alley behind The Green Fairy. Elliot's right hand looked as if it were part wolf, part bear, and—judging by the curved talons extending from his fingertips—part owl.

"Looks like you've grown . . . *a paw.*"

"I think it's because I ate 'the Special.' "

"It looks like the hand of a . . ." The word caught in Leslie's throat.

"A creature," Elliot said.

"What are we going to do?"

Elliot jammed his fist back into his pocket. "My uncle and the others will help us. We've got to find them. Not to mention stop the Chief from turning this whole town into ghorks!"

Leslie cracked her knuckles. "We'd better get started."

There were three settings on the Impressionisticator™:

    1. *Partly Hazy*

    2. *Mostly Indistinct*

    3. *Totally Blurrified!*

Elliot turned it up to full power. Leslie, in her characteristically all-black outfit, became a kind of pale gray haze. Elliot was transformed into a yellowish-green organic blob. Jean-Remy became nothing more than a silver puff of cloud.

With so much activity at the festival, it was easy for them to sneak through the crowds unnoticed. When they left the market square, they found they had to move more slowly to avoid being spotted. When they arrived at the Heppleworth Food Factory, the offices were mostly deserted. The only people there were a handful of security guards. Being *Totally Blurrified!*, they snuck past the security gate with only the merest looks of suspicion.

"What was that?" they heard one of the guards say to his partner.

"What was what?"

"Something just blew past us."

"Aw, you're seeing things," said the other.

"Something just ran by the guardhouse, I swear!"

"Oh, yeah? What'd it look like?"

"Like a . . . like a . . . hmm . . . maybe you're right. I'll get my eyes checked."

The lobby of the spoon building had been cordoned off with pylons and construction barriers, which made it appear that the wreckage caused by the crash of the Coleopter-copter was nothing more than an ongoing renovation. Sadly, there was no sign of the flying machine itself. Elliot assumed the ghorks had torn poor Hercules to shreds. They skirted around the barriers and headed for the Heppleworth expectavators.

"You know what?" Leslie whispered to Elliot. "If we stand still, this really *is* like being invisible."

"Maybe being invisible isn't about people not seeing you," he answered, "it's about people not *noticing* you."

"In zis way," whispered Jean-Remy, with a note of sadness, "ze world is full of invisible people."

When they called the expectavator, it too was deserted. Leslie and Elliot were a little disappointed not to find Sunny, the spring-heeled optimistimonster, waiting for them on his bounding leg.

"Which button do we press?" Elliot asked.

There were so many. *Wilted Hydrangea beside the Water Cooler in the Accounting Department. Heppleworth's Organic Vegetable Soup-Stirring Machine. Northeast Corner of the Packaging Plant behind the Broken Shrink-Wrapper.* Then there was the whole section devoted entirely to dungeons. *Dungeon #1, Dungeon #2, Dungeon #3,* and on and on. But there were so many! Which one was the right one? Which one would lead them to their friends? At last, Jean-Remy hovered up to a few buttons improbably mounted in the ceiling.

"What about zis one? It says *Secret.*"

"Secret what?" asked Elliot.

"Secret nothing. Just *Secret.* If you have kidnapped not only one *but two* creature departments, would you not want to keep it a secret? What greater secret zan zis could ze ghorks be hiding?"

"He has a point," said Elliot.

Leslie wasn't convinced. "How can it be secret if they have a *button* for it?"

"It *is* on the ceiling," Elliot suggested.

"Fine," said Leslie. "Press it, and we'll hope for the best."

"*Mais bien sûr!*" said Jean-Remy, tapping the button. "Hope is *precisely* what we must do! Expectavators, after all, zey are powered by hope, so let us try to be as *hopeful* as possible."

"I hope we find our friends," said Elliot. "I hope Gügor found his true love, I hope there's no such thing as a Sixth Ghork, and I hope we can stop the Chief from turning everyone at the festival into ghorks."

"I hope I can get an autograph from Boris Minor and every one of the Karloffs," said Leslie. "Oh, and I hope my grandpa comes back!"

DA-DING!

The doors opened on a deserted tunnel. It was taller and broader than the one that had led them to Dr. Heppleworth. The walls were smoother, and the floor had been swept . . . or perhaps it was simply well-traveled, its dust kicked away by marching feet. There seemed to be even fewer luster bugs to light the interior, so vast, quavering shadows haunted every surface.

Elliot and Leslie strained their eyes to peer into the tunnel, but it was no use. Its depths quickly faded to an indecipherable darkness. What so-called "secret" awaited them at the other end, they wondered.

As they tiptoed along the tunnel, they smelled something. It was a salt-and-peppery and (almost) appetizing odor, but there was something *vague* about it. It was as if the scent had been made hazy by an olfactory version of the Impressionisticator™.

At last, they arrived on a balcony overlooking a large space very much like the laboratory at the DENKi-3000 Creature Department. There was machinery everywhere: cogs and gears; buttons and switches; dials and readouts; cables and chains and countless conveyors. However, unlike the Creature Department, where it always seemed like there were a hundred different projects and experiments going on, this room had only one. Every cog, button, and conveyor was dedicated to a single purpose.

Making food.

Eerily, there was no one here. Everything was automated. Monstrous articulated claws stirred huge vats of raw ingredients—vegetables and meats and grains and seasonings. The mixtures sluiced through pipes into blazing ovens.

"Why do I feel like I'm in the belly of giant robot—with stomach flu?" asked Elliot.

"Because zat is exactly what it looks like," said Jean-Remy.

Finally, trays emerged from the ovens with meals that looked disturbingly familiar.

"Is it just me," said Leslie, "or is there something weird about those TV dinners? Don't you think they look like—"

"*Faces!*" said Elliot. They had seen one just like it before. "They all look like a 'Special' from The Smiling Mudsucker."

"Zees must be what Quazicom and ze ghorks think ze manufacture of food ought to be. Speaking for ze French, it is appalling!"

"Come on," said Elliot. "If we're going to find my uncle and the others, we should keep moving." He pointed farther down, to a dim glow of light leaking into the end of the passageway.

They tiptoed along, having no idea where they were headed but confident that, thanks to being *Totally Blurrified!*, no one would spot them.

The tunnel rose up in a slope toward a huge, underground coliseum, teeming with ghorks. Staying close to the rear wall, they tiptoed into the chamber. All the ghorks had their attention focused on a plateau of stone at the center. On this platform, seated all in a row, were the Five Head Ghorks: Iris, Adenoid Jack, Wingnut, Digits, and Grinner.

A great black cube hung above them, with a view-screen on each of its four sides. Suddenly, the coliseum was filled with strident, forceful music, like something you might hear before an action-packed news bulletin. All the view-screens flashed to life, showing a stylized Q above the words:

QUAZICOM INC.

TAKING OVER EVERYTHING, ONE COMPANY AT A TIME

The words faded and were replaced with a shadowy face. Its only visible feature was a set of gleaming white teeth. It was the Chief.

"Welcome," he said, in his loose-gravelly voice, "I'm sure you must be as anxious as I am to finally meet the Fabled Sixth Ghork! Weeks ago I sent your faithful leaders—Grinner, Iris, Adenoid Jack, Wingnut, and Digits—to search all of creaturedom to find him, and now, at long last, he is here with us tonight, the ghork who will lead us in victory over the rest of creaturedom!"

A terrible cheer rose from the sea of ghorks.

"Before we begin the proceedings, however, there is a question that needs answering. . . ." Two tiny daggers of light sparkled in his invisible eyes. "*What* is that little girl doing at the back of the room?"

Every ghork in the coliseum turned in their seats and looked directly at Leslie. Leslie, meanwhile, looked down at herself and saw—to her horror—that her blurrification had worn off. When she looked up again, she was surrounded by sneering ghorks.

"Would you believe I'm a cabaret performer?" she asked.

(No, they wouldn't.)

The ghorks grabbed Leslie and pulled her toward the front of the crowd.

"What should we do with her, Chief? You want us to lock

her up with the others?"

The chief shook his head. "Let her stay. I'd like her to witness the terror of the Sixth Ghork!"

Up above Leslie, Jean-Remy's blurrification had also worn off. Before he could flutter away, one of the hand-ghorks leapt up and plucked him out of the air like an insect. Jean-Remy was also pulled forward and given a front-row seat at the Great Hexposé. Only Elliot remained *Totally Blurrified!*

Up on the plateau, Grinner pointed at Leslie. "I know you! You're that girl from the hotel. What happened to your little friend, the dorky kid in the fishing vest?"

"I don't know what you're talking about," Leslie told him. She hoped to give Elliot enough time to slip away unseen. "I haven't seen him since yesterday," she lied. "In fact, I have no idea *where* he is!"

Grinner gritted his teeth and laughed. "What do you think, I'm stupid? When I asked, what happened to him, I didn't mean, where is he? We can all see he's right behind you! What I meant was *what happened to him?*"

Leslie turned around and—

"AAIIIEEEEGH!"

She screamed because, just like she and Jean-Remy, Elliot's blurrification had also worn off. Now that he was visible again, Leslie saw that her friend was no longer the person she remembered. In fact, Elliot didn't look like a person at all.

Elliot was a creature!

CHAPTER 20

In which the five ghorks unveil a Sixth

lliot was a creature. There was no other way to put it. It wasn't just his fingertips that had transformed. It wasn't just his hand. It was *all of him.*

Elliot.

Was.

A creature!

To make matters worse, he was now locked in a cage with Leslie and Jean-Remy, at the front of a coliseum full of ghorks.

Elliot looked down at himself. His hands looked more like *paws*. They bristled with hair like his father's shaving brush (if it was green). His fingers were tipped with dull, twisted talons—and his feet! They were *huge*! They had swollen so big, they had burst clean out of his sensible loafers. When he looked down, he saw only a pair of monstrous green clompers that were half grizzly bear, half *emu*. Three sharp black toes, splayed wide in three directions, poked out from under a shaggy thatch of moss-green hair.

What he wanted most of all was to see his face. When he raised his hand (or rather his *paw*) he felt chisel-sharp cheekbones and nothing but hair. When he opened his mouth he felt a jagged mountain range of teeth. He felt an elongated jaw, almost like a snout. He even felt a cold wet nose, and if he crossed his eyes he could see it, a distracting black blob. *Is this what* a dog *sees everywhere it goes?* he wondered. *Or a yeti?* One thing was for sure: His glasses didn't fit properly anymore. They kept slipping sideways. If only he had a mirror!

"My face," he whispered to Leslie. "What does it look like?"

"Let me say this," she replied. "At least you didn't turn into a ghork."

"Okay, but then *what am I?*"

"I think you look quite dashing," said Jean-Remy, "and zat is a great compliment coming from someone as impeccably handsome as myself."

Elliot sighed. "I think we have *very* different definitions of handsome."

"You know," said Leslie, "you actually look a bit like the original drummer from Boris Minor and the Karloffs. He left the band after their second album."

"Is that supposed to make me feel better?"

"He was a *really* good drummer."

Elliot threw up his hands. "But everyone in that band is dressed up like *a spook!*"

Leslie nodded. "Think of it this way. You look like . . . *a rock star!*"

"Boris Minor and the Karloffs are *not* the kind of rock stars I'm into."

"Are you into *any* rock stars?"

"Can't you just *pleeease* describe what I look like?"

Leslie took a deep breath. "Like the world's dorkiest werewolf —and probably the greenest."

Elliot adjusted his glasses. "Not cool."

"It could be the vest," said Leslie.

"What?"

"I know you're not going to like this," Leslie told him, "but maybe you'd look better without the fishing vest."

Elliot regarded his friend suspiciously. "Why am I not surprised to hear you say that?"

"I'm being serious," Leslie told him.

Elliot looked down at himself. "But I *never* take it off."

"Don't tell me you sleep in it!"

Elliot shrugged. "Sometimes. If I'm really tired."

"You love it *that much*?"

Elliot nodded gamely.

Leslie threw up her arms. "A bright green fishing vest? Seriously?! Can you really not tell it's the single most dorky article of clothing any twelve-year-old in the complete history of all possible twelve-year-olds *has ever worn*?"

Elliot *did* have a vague idea that some people thought his fishing vest was a little—well, dorky. But Leslie was his friend. She couldn't really think . . .

"You hate it, don't you?"

Leslie winced. "I just think you should take it off once in a while."

"You really think I'd look better if I did?"

Leslie hesitated before she answered. "I just think it might clash with your new look. Very few people can pull off green-on-green."

Elliot fiddled with the zipper on his fishing vest. Slowly, inch by agonizing inch, he pulled it down. Then he slipped out of his most prized piece of clothing. For a moment, he hugged the shapeless fabric to his chest like it was a baby. *His* baby. Then, very slowly, he folded it (with the utmost care, of course) and stowed it away in his knapsack.

"What do you think?" he asked. He rolled up the sleeves of his yellow rugby shirt and spread his hairy green arms. "Better?"

Leslie squinted at him. She looked just about to say something, when she was interrupted by Grinner, who rose from his seat and stepped up to the microphone.

The unveiling of the Sixth Ghork had begun.

"*In the beginning,* we ghorks were nothing more than a ragtag bunch of ogres-slash-trolls-slash-overgrown gremlins, aimlessly wandering around our secret underground lairs without any real sense of purpose. Back in those days, there was very little to set us apart from any old ogre, troll, or overgrown gremlin. But then something happened. One of our ancestors was born . . . *a little different.*"

There was a smattering of cheers from the crowd.

Grinner glanced over at Adenoid Jack. "Maybe that first little ghork's *nose* was just a little bigger than the others."

Adenoid Jack pointed two fingers at his schnoz and then pumped one fist in the air. The nose-ghorks hollered and snorted.

"Or perhaps," Grinner went on, "it was the *ears* that stuck out. Or the *eyes.* Or the *hands.*" With each reference to a new sense, Grinner looked to one of his compatriots, and cheers erupted from the appropriate segment of the crowd. When the cheers of the hand-ghorks died down, Grinner smiled. "Then again, maybe that little ghork was born with a big . . . *mouth.*"

There was a boom of cheering from the mouth-ghorks.

"Whichever it was, that small difference set that ghork apart, and so began a grand tradition! It not only defines who we are as ghorks but is the very thing that has brought us here today. *Today* is the day we fulfill an ancient Ghorkolian prophecy! Because today, the five Ghorkolian tribes . . . *become six*!"

These words received the loudest cheer of all. On the viewscreen, even the Chief was clapping his shadowy hands.

"Of course," Grinner went on, "there were those who didn't believe the Fabled Sixth Ghork existed. They said it was a myth! An impossible dream! But the five of us—*the Five Ghorks*—we never gave up. We searched and searched, scouring the twenty-three corners of creaturedom, until one day . . ." Grinner spread out his arms, looking to the far edge of the plateau. ". . .we found what we were looking for."

Elliot and Leslie watched as five young ghorks (one from each tribe) walked up the slope to the plateau, carrying with them a great black palanquin. It was a wooden box like the passenger compartment of an engineless taxicab. The exterior was ornately carved and topped with a domed cupola roof. Four carrying poles protruded from its corners. Each was settled on the shoulders of four of the ghorks, while the fifth, a willowy hand-ghork, followed behind.

The palanquin's dark wood looked as if were charred, like something scavenged from the dead trees of a forest fire. Thick red curtains hung inside the windows, so it was impossible to see inside.

The four ghorks marched slowly to the center of the plateau, where they set the palanquin down. There was a crack of electricity as a spotlight lanced through the air. It illuminated a bright white circle directly in front of the palanquin's door. Next, one of the hand-ghorks grasped the handle. He froze in that position, waiting.

Grinner leaned forward, his teeth nearly clicking against the microphone, and whispered, "And now . . . to lead us all in ultimate victory, I proudly present . . . *the Sixth Ghork*!"

The coliseum fell absolutely silent. The palanquin door was pulled open. Behind it, a velvet curtain billowed. Then . . .

The Fabled Sixth Ghork stepped into the spotlight.

"He's shorter than I expected," Leslie whispered.

It was true. The Sixth Ghork wasn't terribly impressive. He was rather small, even compared to the smallest of ghorks. In fact, he wasn't much taller than Elliot himself, but perhaps that was because he was so young. He had the mottled green skin of a ghork, but none of their obscenely enlarged features. He didn't have a big pointy nose, or a big slavering mouth, or big bulging eyes, or big floppy ears. He didn't even have enormous hands. In a freakish, ogre/troll/overgrown gremlin sort of way, he looked quite ordinary.

Also unlike the other ghorks, whose expressions ranged invariably between a sour scowl and a bitter sneer, the Sixth Ghork's face was expressionless. He almost looked bored.

It was only when Elliot's eyes traveled down to the floor that he saw what set him apart.

His feet!

"They're *huge*," Elliot whispered.

Not only were they enormous, but (again, unlike all the others) the Sixth Ghork was wearing shoes. They were bright red, high-cut dress shoes, with blue stars on the outsides of each ankle and a yellow checkered pattern over their bulbous toes.

"Everyone," said Grinner, "I'd like you to meet Giggles."

"Hold on a minute," said the Chief, who didn't sound terribly impressed. "Did you say—"

"*Giggles,*" Grinner repeated in an ominous tone.

"Why are you saying it like that?"

"Because that's his name." Grinner raised his hands and fluttered them like ghosts. "*Giiiiiiiiggles!*"

"The Fabled Sixth Ghork," said the Chief, "is called . . . *Giggles*?"

"Exactly!" cried Grinner.

The Chief folded his arms. "It's not the sort of name that strikes fear into the hearts of one's enemies."

"I wasn't finished," said Grinner. "You see, Giggles is called 'Giggles' because he has an amazing sixth sense that no other ghork in the world possesses . . . *a sense of humor*!"

The vast crowd of ghorks *ooh*ed and *aah*ed in wonderment.

"A sense of humor?" said Elliot.

"Definitely not what I was expecting," said Leslie.

The Chief of Quazicom agreed. "*A sense of humor?!*" he boomed. "I bankrolled expeditions to all twenty-three corners of creaturedom, and *this* is what you bring me?! You do know I had to murder three of my best accountants just to get funding approval!"

"B-but, Mr. Chief, sir," Grinner sputtered. "We looked everywhere! You gotta believe us, this most definitely is—"

"Mind-reading! Predicting the future! Telekinesis! *That's* what people mean when they talk about a sixth sense!"

"*Aha!*" said Grinner. He flashed a triumphant smile at the Chief's looming shadow. "Maybe that's what *people* say, but we're talking about ghorks here. And this is Giggles. He comes with a *Ghorkolian* sense of humor!"

"Is that supposed to impress me?"

"Of course! Just look at him!" Grinner pointed at Giggles.

"Look at his face. Expressionless! *Utterly expressionless!* Do you know what that means?"

"No," said the Chief. "Should I?"

"Lemme explain," said Grinner. "You see, Giggles here *never laughs*. He never even cracks a smile. That's because he has the driest, most dour sense of humor in the world. *Nothing in the known universe* is capable of making Giggles giggle! Amazing, huh?"

The Chief buried his shadowy face in his shadowy hands. "I don't believe it. I blew *three years* of Quazicom's research and development budget on this. *This!* A weasely little ghork in clown shoes! I swear, I'll have to take over five new companies this year alone, just to make up the shortfall!" He glared out at the sea of ghorks. "I'm sorry, but you guys *really* need to work on your ancient Ghorkolian prophecies. This is unacceptable!"

"B-but, Chief! Mr. Chief! Sir! *Your highness!* You have to—"

"No, I don't! You'll just have to go back out there and keep looking. I don't care if you have to bring me back a Fabled *Seventh* Ghork, but please—bring me something I can work with. *An extremely dry sense of humor?* You expect us to take over creaturedom with an extremely dry sense of humor?"

"B-but, sir . . ." stammered Grinner, uncharacteristically at a loss for words.

"Listen, Chief," said Iris, rising from her chair. "What Grinner's trying to say is, don't be too hasty." She put out one hand, gesturing toward the Fabled Sixth Ghork. "What could be more insidious than a creature so profoundly evil he is utterly devoid of even the merest modicum of mirth? Isn't that just the sort of spiteful, maniacally devious ghork we need to lead us?"

In the spotlight, Giggles yawned.

"Well," said the Chief, "when you put it that way, it actually makes a bit of sense." He gave his shadowy chin a thoughtful rub. "Yes, you might have a point. But first, I'll need a test."

"A t-test?" asked Iris. She suddenly sounded much less confident than a moment ago.

"Of course," said the Chief. "I need to determine exactly how truly humorless Giggles is."

"How are you going to do that?"

"By telling him a joke," said the Chief.

"But sir, you can't really be—"

"*Ssh!* I've got a good one." The Chief cleared his throat and looked down at Giggles. "Why is it," he asked, "that eye-ghorks are so gullible?"

"Hey!" said Iris, obviously offended.

"Because," said the Chief, "*seeing* is believing!"

Ghorks all across the coliseum burst out laughing—all except the eye-ghorks, of course. They sat glumly silent, just as offended as Iris.

"That's a *terrible* joke," said Leslie, rolling her eyes.

Jean-Remy agreed. "Only ze ghorks—creatures without ze sense of humor—could laugh at such a ridiculous pun!"

Giggles, however, wasn't laughing. He hadn't so much as twitched.

"You see?" said Grinner, finding his voice again. "It's impossible to make him laugh!"

But the Chief had more, one for each kind of ghork:

"Why do ear-ghorks hate Day-Glo T-shirts? Because the colors are *too loud*!"

"Why do nose-ghorks hate people who complain a lot? Because they can't stand it when people kick up *a stink*!"

"Why are hand-ghorks scared of being sent to an insane asylum? Because it means they've *lost touch* with reality!"

"Why are mouth-ghorks so bad at doing their taxes? Because there's *no accounting for taste*!"

Each joke was rewarded in the same way: with laughter and cheering from four fifths of the ghorks (the ones who weren't the butt of the joke) and no reaction at all from Giggles.

At last, when the Chief ran out of gags, Grinner smiled triumphantly. "See?" he said. "You couldn't do it."

Iris nodded. "Only the most evil of creatures could resist such hilarity!"

"Are you kidding? That wasn't hilarity! Those were the lamest jokes ever!"

"*Who said that?!*" growled the Chief.

"I did," said Leslie. "Down here! In the cage!"

"As far as I'm aware," said the Chief, "we aren't currently seeking input from *people in cages*."

"Well, maybe you should," said Leslie. "At least we *have* a sense of humor, which is probably why we can tell those jokes were *terrible*! I'll bet if your Fabled Sixth Ghork heard something that was *actually funny*, he'd crack up just like anybody else would."

"Oh, really?" asked the Chief. "All right, then. Let's hear one."

Leslie squinted up at him. "One what?"

"*One joke.* Something that—as you so eloquently put it—is actually funny." The Chief spoke with such gravity it was clear there would be consequences if Leslie didn't come up with something hilarious. Every eye in the room (some of them repulsively huge) swiveled to the cage.

"Umm . . ." said Leslie. "Let me see. . . ."

Silence fell across the coliseum. The Chief leaned forward in his executive captain's chair, and the creak of leather was so sharp and loud it was like a crash of thunder.

A crash, thought Elliot. *That's it!*

He jumped up and waved his hairy, creaturely arm through the bars. "I know!" he cried. "I know something so funny, it's *guaranteed* to make Giggles giggle."

The Chief turned his attention from Leslie to Elliot. "And who might you be?"

"I'm Elliot."

"That's strange, you don't look like an Elliot. What sort of creature are you?"

"I'm a . . . umm . . . *a green-vested fuzzball.*"

"Where's your green vest?"

Elliot looked down at himself. "I took it off because it didn't really go with . . . well, never mind that. Listen, if you really want to test Giggles, you've got to show him something truly hilarious, and I know just the thing!"

"Oh, really?"

Elliot nodded. He realized this might be his one chance to save the day. If they could make Giggles laugh, the Chief would be convinced the Fabled Sixth Ghork wasn't up to the job of leading an army of ghorks.

"What is it," asked the Chief, "you think is so funny?"

Elliot puffed out his hairy chest. "*My friends*! Or at least their cabaret performance!"

"That's right!" said Leslie. "That was the silliest, funniest thing we've ever seen! It was so hilarious it even crashed a chiropractor!"

"Excuse me?" asked the Chief.

"She means *Coleopter-copter*," said Elliot, "but that's another story. If you let my friends perform in the Simmersville Food Festival Dinner-Theatre-Style Costume Cabaret, we'll prove that Giggles isn't as evil as you think he is. In fact, maybe he's not even the Sixth Ghork at all!"

"*Liar!*" screeched Iris. "Of course he's the Fabled Sixth Ghork! He's the most evil ghork the world has ever known! Just look at him!"

In the spotlight, Giggles blinked.

"How do you know?" asked Elliot. "It's common knowledge there's more than eleven thousand different kinds of creatures in creaturedom! Can you really be sure you found the right one?"

"Mr. Chief, *please*," said Grinner. "You're not *really* going to listen to a . . . to a . . . a *green-vested fuzzball*, are you?"

"Perhaps, my bigmouthed minion," said the Chief, "you're forgetting something. That something is: *I'm the Chief*, and I can listen to whoever I want! And if I find out you brought me the wrong ghork . . . I'm going to be very, very, *very* upset."

Grinner waggled his arms, his huge mouth gaping up at the screen. "But Chief! I'm telling you, we looked everywhere! This is him! Giggles *is* the Fabled Sixth Ghork!"

"Maybe so," said the Chief, "but now—thanks to that green-vested fuzzball down there—we have a way of finding out, *don't we?*" He turned his attention to the cage at the foot of the plateau and smiled in a way that made Elliot shiver.

"Fuzzball," he said, "you got yourself a deal. If you can make Giggles giggle, I'll let everyone go." He turned his attention to the Five Ghorks. "Then you five bozos will go out and find me *the real Sixth Ghork!*"

"B-but, sir!" Grinner stammered. "Th-this is the r-real S-S-Si—"

"Zip it, bigmouth," snapped the Chief. "Tonight we'll settle this in the only way possible. *With cabaret!*"

CHAPTER 21

In which the creatures learn you can't teach old inventions new tricks, Jean-Remy reveals the truth, and Elliot has an idea

hat have you done with Elliot?" asked Professor von Doppler. He stood near the entrance of Dungeon 101, where the ghorks had just deposited three new prisoners: Leslie, Jean-Remy, and a fuzzy green creature in a yellow rugby shirt.

"I *am* Elliot!" said the fuzzy green creature in the yellow rugby shirt.

"From where I'm standing," said Harrumphrey (who was standing next to the professor), "you look more like creature type 887, subset F: a three-toed bristle-imp."

"How do you remember all that?" Leslie asked him.

Harrumphrey responded with a shrug that went directly from his ankles to his chin. "Look at the size of this noggin. Gotta fill it with something!"

"Elliot's telling the truth," Leslie told the professor. "The ghorks did this to him. It's all because he ordered Grinner's 'Special' when we first arrived."

The professor walked around Elliot, examining him closely.

When he arrived back in front of his nephew, he took off his glasses and slapped one hand over his face. "When we get out of this, your parents are going to kill me!"

"Don't worry," said Elliot. "Now that we're all back together, I'm sure we'll figure out a way to turn me back to normal—using creature science, of course!"

"I'm *sss*orry," said an eerie, slurring voice behind Elliot, "but that'*sss* not going to happen."

Elliot turned around to see the small dark caverns that adjoined the main dungeon. The voice had come from inside them. Emerging from the darkness, there came a huge green lizard, a creature that was half python and half crocodile, with a mouthful of jigsaw teeth and huge glossy eyes. Its long sinuous tail swished as it walked, and its shimmering green scales glimmered in the flickering light.

Scales, thought Elliot. *Green scales!*

"You're the clerk from the Simmersville Inn!" Leslie blurted.

The lizard nodded sadly. She was dressed in only the tatters of her former uniform, but over her heart, clipped to the remains of her shirt, was a name tag:

Hello, my name is Emily.

"I gue*sss* you ordered the *Sssss*pecial," she said to Elliot.

He nodded. "You said turning us back is impossible. Why?"

"There'*sss* no antidote," Emily hissed. "Even if one existed, it would have to be cooked with exactly the same ingredient*sss*s as the original dis*ss*h. But *sss*adly, that awful *sss*chef merely threw in whatever was lying around the kitchen, so no one knows the re*sssc*ipe, not even him."

"Grinner!" Elliot muttered. He despised the mouth-ghork more than ever before. "You mean we can't change back? Not ever?"

Emily shook her head. "None of u*sss* can."

"There's more of you?" asked Leslie.

Emily nodded. Behind her, emerging from the same cavern, came four more creatures. First, a beast like a bright green polar bear; then another creature who resembled a fastidious businessman, only with a long green neck and the bovine head of a giraffe; third, a creature like a stooping four-armed troll (also green); and a creature with only one eye, extending on a mossy tendril above a body that was almost entirely stomach. Each of them wore pitiful expressions of fear and bewilderment.

"They turned all of you into creatures?" asked Elliot.

The emerald-green polar bear creature nodded. "They call us 'the Specimens.'"

"I'm afraid Emily's right," said the professor. He placed one hand on Elliot's hairy shoulder. "We've been locked in here since yesterday, and we've tried everything we know to change them back. But without Grinner's recipe, it's impossible."

Elliot looked down at his paws, at his talons, at his ungainly feet. He was a three-toed bristle-imp, and he was going to stay that way. As the certainty of this sunk in, he felt his heart thump faster and his breath catch in his throat. Ever since he had left Bickleburgh, he had wondered about the possibility that perhaps he belonged to creaturedom. Now his wish had been granted . . . and he only felt dizzy. He could hardly breathe.

"This . . . ," he gasped, "is going to take some getting used to." He looked up at his friends. "Please, can somebody give me a mirror?"

Unfortunately, dungeons weren't the sorts of places where

fine grooming was terribly important. The closest anyone could find to a mirror was a brass flywheel, but it was far too tarnished to offer Elliot a clear reflection. All he saw was a cloudy, greenish smudge, as if he were still *Totally Blurrified!*

As Elliot stood in silence, trying (and failing) to see what he looked like, he suddenly became aware of a flurry of activity all around him. He looked up to see the creatures of DENKi-3000 actively engaged in building things, tinkering with strange apparatuses, conducting arcane experiments, just as if they were at home in the Creature Department.

"What's everyone doing?" Leslie asked.

"Believe it or not," said the professor, "they're trying to build weapons."

"*Weapons?*" asked Jean-Remy. "But look! Zat . . . *zat is my flying pan!*"

Patti Mudmeyer was across the dungeon, holding a remote control. She used it to steer what was obviously a prototype of Jean-Remy's invention (a conventional frying pan with flapping, mechanical wings). A short distance away, Reggie stood stoically straight, his hands on his hips, as the flying pan swatted and spanked him about the head and shoulders. Unfortunately, since the great bombastadon was so blubbery, the blows had very little effect.

"No, no, no!" cried Jean-Remy. "Blasphemy! You have it all wrong! What is more, you are not even cooking ze crêpe! You are just beating ze bombastadon!" He soared over to Patti, and the two of them began wrestling over the remote.

Meanwhile, at another table, several of Harrumphrey's shoe-horn horns had been arranged on tripods, with their speakers pointed at Gabe, the mildly depressed DENKi-3000 expectavator operator, who sat slumped in a chair nearby. The shoehorn horns played "When the Saints Go Marching In" at top volume, but the sound quality was poor and tinny. It did little more than make Gabe tap his listless foot in time with the melody.

Then there was a table where Bildorf and Pib were strapped to a pair of miniature hospital gurneys. Above them, a suspended lightbulb flashed on and off, its glass casing printed with a ghoulish face. When the light switched on, the face said, "Boo!"

On.

"Boo!"

"GAH!"

Off.

On.

"Boo!"

"ERK!"

Off . . .

And so on. This was obviously a prototype of Patti's invention, the Fright Bulb. Although it had the effect of startling the two hobmongrels, it was hardly very menacing.

"Those are the worst weapons I've ever seen," said Elliot.

"Weapons aren't really our forte," said the professor.

"Why are they trying to turn perfectly good inventions into weapons in the first place?" asked Leslie.

"We don't have a choice. I'll show you why."

The professor led them past laboratory tables where creatures tried in vain to make weaponry (and where Jean-Remy still battled Patti for control of his flying pan). They left this first part of the dungeon and entered another cavern, and then another. Elliot recalled the paradoxes of creature physics, the fact that rooms (or in this case, *locked cells*) could be larger than they first appeared. He began to wonder if a dungeon like this could go on . . . *forever.*

At last, they turned down a passage that grew narrower and narrower until it contracted to a cramped dead end. At the center of the final wall was a small, perfectly round circle of light. It was a hole, no bigger than the face of a clock, carved straight through the rock.

"Look through there," said the professor.

Elliot and Leslie each peered through the hole. They saw a completely white room. It was so brightly lit, there seemed to be no floor, ceiling or walls. It was dizzying to stare into such limitless emptiness. Floating in the midst of all that white was something very peculiar: *a gigantic blender.*

One of the ghorks' spherical cages hung above it, suspended from a thick chain like a hideous Christmas ornament. The chain rose up and up and up until it became nothing but a thin black thread, vanishing into the snow-white emptiness above. Inside the cage were three figures. The first was—

"Gügor!" Leslie cried.

She shouted the word, but the sound was swallowed up by the strange acoustics of the white chamber. Gügor couldn't hear her. The big knucklecrumpler lay flat on his back, and he looked awful. Cuts and bruises covered his body. Standing over him was a second, much smaller figure. It was a toad-like creature in a ratty cardigan. He peered down at Gügor with a look of pity and concern.

"Dr. Heppleworth," said Elliot.

"You know him?" asked the professor.

"We met," Elliot explained, "when we first came down here to meet you."

The third figure was the smallest of all, hovering in the air only inches above Gügor's head. A beautiful fairy-bat. She was gently stroking his colorful dreadlocks and singing to him in a whispered voice.

"That's her, isn't it?" Elliot asked. "Jean-Remy's sister."

"Gügor's One True Love," said Leslie.

"Yes," said the professor. "So you see we have no choice but to obey the Chief. If we don't invent him some sort of ultimate weapon, he'll grind up Gügor and feed whatever comes out to the mouth-ghorks."

"That's awful!" Leslie cried.

"That's the Chief," said Elliot.

"The same goes for Dr. Heppleworth and Eloise-Yvette. The Chief is using them to force the Food Factory Creature Department to create something even worse."

"A secret potion," said Leslie.

"That'll turn the whole town into ghorks," said Elliot.

The professor nodded.

"Wait a second," said Leslie. She stooped to look through the hole one more time. "There's something I don't get. Jean-Remy told us his sister was selfish and vain and couldn't be trusted, but she looks like the sweetest, gentlest creature I've ever seen! How can that be her?"

"It is," said a voice they hadn't expected to hear. "Zat is her."

Leslie drew her face away from the wall and saw Jean-Remy floating above them. He had obviously followed them down into this part of the dungeon.

"Leslie's right," Elliot said to him. "She doesn't seem anything like you described."

"It is possible," Jean-Remy admitted, "I *may* have exaggerated her negative traits."

"What happened between you two?" asked Leslie.

Jean-Remy fluttered down to the hole and peeked through. He was silent for a moment. Then he clutched his heart and whispered, "Ah, yes . . . *Bernard*. Hello, my old friend."

"Bernard?" asked the professor. "Who's Bernard?"

"It's not a who," Leslie reminded him. "It's a *what*. 'Bernard' is what Jean-Remy calls the embodiment of his heartache. It's a love he once lost. Giving it a name is how he deals with it."

Professor nodded. "Very wise, in a creaturely way."

"Is that why you and your sister don't get along?" Elliot asked Jean-Remy. "Does it have something to do with . . . 'Bernard'?"

"It has *everything* to do with Bernard." Jean-Remy floated away from the wall. "It was long ago, and, like Gügor in his cage, I was in love. . . ."

Jean-Remy explained that, in his youth, he had been in love with a full-blooded fairy princess named Luna. Of course, being only a humble fairy-bat, the princess's father (a proud fairy king, of course) would never accept his daughter's love for, as he put it, "a ragamuffin mongrel." He banished Jean-Remy from his kingdom, forbidding the fairy-bat to ever see his daughter again.

Distraught, Jean-Remy enlisted the aid of Eloise-Yvette. Her shimmering beauty meant she was often mistaken for a full-blooded fairy. Even amid the towers of a fairy palace, she could pass unnoticed. Jean-Remy asked his sister to deliver a note to Princess Luna. In it, he asked the princess to meet him at the tip of the Eiffel Tower at midnight, so they could run away together. To make sure the letter was received, he made Eloise-Yvette promise she would deliver it personally.

"All night long, I waited," muttered Jean-Remy. "Shivering in ze cold wind, at ze very tip-top of ze City of Light! But Luna did not come." Jean-Remy's pale face flushed a subtle shade of red. "Zat is how I know my so-called sister did not follow my instructions. If Luna had truly been given my letter, I know she would have come to join me. She was, after all, as Gügor would say, my 1TL."

"Maybe," said Elliot, looking down at his fuzzy green paws. "Things don't always work out like you plan."

But Jean-Remy didn't want to hear this. "No! My Luna would have come. I *know* she would have come! You see, I discovered zat ze very same night, Eloise-Yvette, she had an audition at ze top jazz club in ze catacombs! I am certain she merely tossed my letter under ze palace door and fluttered off without a word."

Leslie narrowed her eyes. "How do you know that's what happened?"

Jean-Remy shrugged. "It *must* have. Otherwise, Luna would have come, you see?"

"It sounds to me," said Leslie, "like *you're* the one being selfish."

"*Me?!*" Jean-Remy's face flashed with shock.

"Yes, *you*. She's family, Jean-Remy. *She's your sister.* The least you could have done was wait for her to give you an explanation."

Jean-Remy considered this for a moment. At last, he said, "You may be right." He fluttered back to the hole in the wall, peering into the strange white chamber.

"*Jean-Remy!*" cried Eloise-Yvette, seeing her brother's face. She flew to the bars of the cage and called to him. "I'm so glad you are safe! There is something I need to tell you, something important, and it is simply this: I miss you, brother! I'm sorry if things did not work out in Paris, but I want us to be family again. Do you think this is possible?"

"Yes, of course it is," Jean-Remy answered. He turned and smiled at Leslie. "I have just realized zat I am ze one who ought to apologize. It was rash of me to leave Paris without a word. What does it matter if you ran off to your audition and did not give my letter to Luna? I should have waited to speak to you before I left. Instead, I carried such heartbreak, such resentment, for such a long time."

Eloise-Yvette furrowed her brow. "*Run off? To an audition?* I never ran off to any audition."

Now it was Jean-Remy who looked confused. "But I assumed zat was why Luna did not come. You did not put my letter *in her hand*, as I asked."

"That's exactly what I did," said Eloise-Yvette. "I did everything you asked. I snuck into the palace, I saw her myself, I gave her the letter."

"So . . . she did receive it after all." Jean-Remy was already as pale as the moon, but when his sister told him this, he turned even whiter. "And yet, she did not come."

"I'm sorry," said Eloise-Yvette.

Jean-Remy looked terribly disappointed. He opened his mouth as if to say something, but he was interrupted by a loud crash from the main part of the dungeon. A moment later, Patti came running into the chamber, her seaweed hair splashing briny muck in every direction.

"Doc!" she said to the professor. "You'd better come quick."

"What is it, Patti?" he asked.

"It's the two Creature Departments," she said. "They're having themselves one heckuva fight. And guess who started it!"

CHAPTER 22

In which Reggie picks a fight, and an unusual transformation occurs

Harrumphrey grappled with a triple-bearded oven troll. Bildorf and Pib wrestled with a pair of ankle snypes. Patti Mudemeyer slung gooey hair-sludge at a flock of mini-gryffs. Cosmo Clutch took on a marrowwrangler singlehand-edly (a rare feat). And even Gabe swiped limply at a slobberwolf, when it tried to drown him in spit.

At the center of everything was Colonel-Admiral Reginald T. Pusslegut, with the two hobmongrels, Bildorf and Pib, cling-ing to his uniform for dear life.

"Over my cold and slippery corpse, I say! Over my *cold and slippery corpse*!" Reggie appeared to be battling his way through all the rest of the creatures at once, regardless of whose side they were on. (To be fair, in light of the chaos engulfing Dungeon 101, it was impossible to even tell if there *were* any sides.) "If you patrolled the tunnels as I have," Reggie went on, slapping a four-eyed snood full in the face, "then you would know—all too well—that we've already got more than enough of those beastly, insufferable, *mucilaginous* cretins as it is!"

"But we don't have a choice," squealed one of the ankle

snypes from the Heppleworth Food Factory. "They're going to grind up Eloise-Yvette—not to mention our beloved CEO!"

"*NO*," Reggie boomed, "I won't have it! A bombastadon *never* colludes with the enemy! It goes against everything he stands for! Everything he *believes*! It defies the very blubber on his bones!"

"Reggie! STOP!" shouted the professor.

The Colonel-Admiral paused, a chestful of air ballooning his ribs. He was one small huff away from a Belly Bounce Maneuver when he exhaled (and the dungeon filled with the scent of vinegar, herring, and rancid chocolate).

"What's going on here?" asked the professor. "Why is everyone fighting?"

"It's these poor misguided creatures of the Heppleworth Food Factory!" Reggie sniffed. "They've succeeded in creating a most abominable elixir! I might even go as far as to call it *iniquitous*."

The professor looked to the Heppleworth creatures. "Is this true?" he asked them. "You've succeeded? You have the ghorks' secret elixir?"

A triple-bearded oven troll ambled out of the group, a large glass beaker in his hand. Inside, a sickly green fluid slopped back and forth like boiled custard. "It's like I told the bombastadon," said the oven troll. "It's either this . . ." He sloshed the contents of the beaker. "Or they grind up our friends. So you see, we're just like you. We don't have a choice."

Elliot peered through the glass, then looked up at Reggie. "How do you *know* it works?"

Everyone looked at each other.

"Well," said Reggie. "I just assumed that . . ."

"We don't know it works," said the triple-bearded oven troll. "Not yet."

"In that case," said a loose-gravelly voice from up above them, "why don't we give it a test?"

On a large view-screen that overlooked all of Dungeon 101, the Chief's shadowy face materialized.

"Oh, and look," he said, "how convenient! Here comes a new specimen now."

Out beyond the bars of Dungeon 101, Grinner, Iris, and Adenoid Jack came loping along the tunnel. They were dragging someone with them, too, someone Elliot and Leslie recognized.

"C-come on, you g-g-guys," stammered the waiter from The Smiling Mudsucker. He was hobbled with chains, with another set linking his wrists. "A joke's a joke, b-b-but don't you think this is taking the whole Costume Cabaret thing a bit too far?"

"Who told you these were costumes?" snorted Adenoid Jack.

"Of course they are," the waiter professed. "You look ridiculous!"

Iris blinked her enormous eyes. *"Excuse me?"*

"It's true!" the waiter gestured at the three ghorks before him. "Big nose? Big eyes? Big mouth? You three look like *cartoon characters*!"

"Why, you little—!" Adenoid Jack reared his head back and prepared to drown the waiter in snot.

Grinner stopped him. "Plug your sniffer, Jack. We're not done with him yet."

"Thanks, Chef," said the waiter, speaking to Grinner in a more friendly tone. "And seriously, the costumes really are amazing, but . . . but . . . say, *where are we?*"

They had arrived at the entrance to Dungeon 101.

"What is this place?" asked the waiter, peering into the cavernous dungeon. For an instant, as he first laid eyes on the creatures, a cloud of fear passed over his face. But it quickly cleared. "Oh! I get it! We're backstage before the big show. This is some kind of dressing room, right?" He shaped his hands into a pair of pistols and shot imaginary bullets of praise into the dungeon. "Like I said, *amazing costumes*, you guys!"

The three ghorks looked at each other and rolled their eyes (especially Iris).

Grinner beamed down at the poor man with a conniving smile. "Tell you what," he said. "You sample one last dish of mine and we'll let you go, okay?"

The waiter looked relieved. "Um . . . okay."

Grinner peered into the dungeon. His eyes landed squarely on the triple-bearded oven troll, the one holding the beaker. "Hand it over, bub."

The oven troll, his knobbly hands trembling, was just about to pass the beaker through the bars, when a big blubbery fist snatched it away.

It was Reggie. "No!" he cried. "I said it once, and I'll say it again!"

"That's the story of his life," Bildorf quipped. He made his hand into a little puppet mouth and flapped his fingers. "Blah, blah, blah, blah, blah, blah, blah . . ."

Reggie ignored Bildorf and waved the beaker high in the air, well out of the reach of any nearby creatures. "I resolutely *refuse* to hand it over!" he bellowed. "For a regimental, not to mention *highly decorated*, bombastadon such as myself to knowingly act in concert with my enemy's wishes is inconceivable! Unimaginable! *Indefensible!*"

"Does he always talk like that?" asked the Chief of Quazicom. Pib nodded. "Always!"

"How do you even get anything done? With that much hot air, I would have had him fired ages ago. Or worse."

"That's because you're totally evil," said Leslie.

"Thank you," said the Chief. "Speaking of being totally evil, why don't we remind our buttery, blubbery, bewhiskered friend here just how truly evil I can be!" Suddenly, the view-screen fizzled with spots and faded to an image of the cage containing Gügor, Eloise-Yvette, and Dr. Heppleworth. The angle was from above, so the mouth of the blender over which they were suspended was clear to see. The countless blades glinted and twitched, and with a terrible grinding whir, they began to spin.

"No!" shouted Elliot.

The shadow of the Chief returned. "Tell your friend," the Chief told him, "to give up the elixir."

Elliot looked at Reggie, who still held the beaker high above his head. His thick arm, however, was trembling. "You, sir," he said to the image of the Chief, "are utterly without honor."

"Finally," said the Chief. "He gets it."

"An enemy without honor is no enemy," Reggie muttered. "An enemy without honor is a beast."

The Chief shrugged. "Beast, enemy. To-may-to, to-mah-to. Just give us the elixir already."

Reluctantly, Reggie passed it through the bars.

"Seriously," said the waiter. "Great show and all, but I really need to get back to work, so—"

"Shut your cake hole, *specimen*," said Adenoid Jack.

"Wait," said Iris. "Don't you want him to *open* his cake hole? How're we gonna feed him the elixir if his mouth's closed?"

"Good point," said Grinner. "*Open* your cake hole!"

"I'd really rather not," said the waiter, grimacing at the awful green slime inside the beaker.

"Suit yourself," said Iris. "We'll open it for you." She gripped the man's head and pried open his mouth. Grinner stood over him and poured a single drip of the horrid solution onto the man's tongue.

The waiter shuddered and retched. He looked like he wanted to vomit, but it was too late. His terrifying transformation had begun. The waiter spun round and covered his face, screaming as his whole body erupted in green blotches. The bones under his skin poked and wriggled and crawled like insects into hideous new places where they had no business to be. He grew taller and broader, and his spine creaked forward into the hunched posture of . . . *a ghork*.

Finally, when he turned to face the others, Elliot saw that what had changed most of all was his nose. It was enormous. The waiter who had once looked haughtily down his nose at Elliot had become a nose-ghork!

"Welcome to the family," said Adenoid Jack.

Slowly, the waiter raised a hand to his face. When he felt his nose, his eyes popped wide. In that moment, he finally understood none of the creatures around him were people in costumes. They were a bunch of crazy monsters! This was too much for the waiter to take in all at once, which was why he started to cry.

"You'll get used to it," Adenoid Jack assured him.

"Excellent," said the Chief. "It's just as I planned! Soon, everyone in Simmersville will be transformed into a fine Ghorkolian soldier, just like . . ." The Chief paused. The waiter didn't look much like soldier material.

In fact, the former waiter wasn't even listening. His eyes rolled up toward the ceiling, and he stumbled sideways as if he were drunk. Elliot, Leslie, and many of the creatures thought he might faint then and there. But he didn't. Instead, he howled. He threw out his arms and shrieked a great sob of sickly green anguish.

Unfortunately, because he had just transformed into a *nose-ghork*, the sob was not without consequences. His crying caused him to empty the incredible contents of his hefty new nostrils. Two gushing torrents of snot blasted to the floor, striking it with such force the ex-waiter was knocked clean off his feet.

"*Oof!*"

He thumped down in a puddle of his own slime. He pounded the floor in despair, and warm snot splashed in every direction. Grinner, Iris, and Adenoid Jack were splattered with the stuff.

"It's all salty!" screeched Iris. "It's stinging my eyes!"

"Calm down already," Adenoid Jack pointed to his own gigantic schnoz as an example. "It's not gonna stop if you keep blubbering!"

The waiter kept blubbering.

"That's enough!" said Grinner. "Get up, crybaby. We'll take you to meet your new family."

They moved as if to drag the newly formed ghork away, but they couldn't. He was blubbering too much, which meant there was way too much snot everywhere. Grinner, Iris, and Adenoid Jack slipped and slopped in it, landing in a messy heap. Meanwhile, the former waiter didn't want to be dragged *anywhere*. When the others tried to grab him, he fought back, kicking and slapping with blows that were as fierce as they were slimy.

From beyond the bars of Dungeon 101, Elliot, Leslie and the

captive creatures watched all of this with a mixture of horror and (obviously) *disgust*.

At last, shrieking his loudest howl yet, the former waiter leapt over his captors and ran thumping into the darkness of the tunnel.

"Well," said Adenoid Jack, flicking a hefty glop of mucus from his fingertips. "That didn't turn out like we planned."

"Let him go," the Chief told the ghorks. "He'll be back once he realizes this is the only place he belongs—with his own kind. Right now, you need to make sure we dribble a drop of that wonderful elixir into every last dish we're serving at the end of the cabaret."

Bowing to his command and flashing a characteristic sneer into Dungeon 101, Grinner led Iris and Adenoid Jack into the tunnels.

"What about Eloise-Yvette," asked the oven troll, "and Dr. Heppleworth? Now that we've done what you asked, you have to let them go."

"Why would you think that?" asked the Chief. He turned his attention to the creatures of DENKi-3000. "I still haven't got my ultimate weapon." He smiled, and the sparkle of his teeth made the rest of his features even murkier. "I'll leave that to you, Professor."

In a fizzle of static, he vanished, and the screen went blank. But before it did, an image appeared. It was almost lost in the flurry of static, but everyone saw it: the ghostly image of a gigantic blender.

CHAPTER 23

In which Elliot and Leslie sketch out something new

lliot's uncle looked very worried. "They're going to feed that stuff to everyone at the festival, right after the cabaret. And unless we come up with some sort of despicable 'ultimate weapon' for the Chief, Gügor gets ground into filling for a Ghorkolian kebab!" He shook his head. "What are we going to do?!"

"The only thing we *can* do," said Elliot. "Perform in the cabaret!"

The professor—and all the creatures—stared at Elliot.

"He's not kidding," said Leslie.

Elliot stepped forward. "Okay, yes, I know this is going to sound weird, but *this is creaturedom*. Weirdness is what we do!" He turned to the professor. "Uncle Archie, aren't you always telling us there's more than one way to save the day? Well . . . that day is today, and we're going to save it in the only way left—with a song-and-dance number!"

Everyone was still staring.

"Seriously," said Leslie. "He's telling the truth."

She and Elliot explained what they had learned: how the Chief was skeptical about Giggles, the so-called Fabled Sixth Ghork, and how, if they could make him laugh in the festival's Dinner-Theatre-Style Costume Cabaret, the Chief would have to start all over again, sending his henchmen out to find another ghork to lead their armies.

"Which means," said Elliot, "if we can make Giggles giggle, *we save the day*!"

Patti Mudmeyer squinted at Elliot. "You think our cabaret performance was that funny?"

"You guys were *hilarious*," Leslie answered. "If there's any-one who can make Giggles giggle, it's all of you."

"I assure you, my friends," said Jean-Remy, "zere was nothing comical in my performance. It was utterly in earnest!"

"Besides, the performance was only meant *as a disguise*," said the professor. "We could never *actually* perform!"

"But I thought you wanted to," said Leslie. "You were cer-tainly excited about it on the way here."

"But that wasn't *the real thing*. It was just for you two!" The professor peeled back his sleeve to check the time. "Anyway, just look! The cabaret is only a few hours off. There's no time to practice."

"Who said anything about practicing?" said Leslie. "It's fun-nier if you don't know what you're doing."

Elliot nodded. "Especially if Reggie goes in for his big finish."

"There is nothing comedic about my submaritone!" said Reggie.

"For once he's right," said Pib. "Not comedic so much as *catastrophic*."

"No-no-no," said Jean-Remy. "Zis is ridiculous! It would

be an insult to ze cabaret if we did not have at least *a teensy* bit of practice. But how can we? Zere is no time! Zat is because ze hardest part of any invention, the part that takes the most time is—what else? *An idea.* Yet we have nothing!"

"We don't even have a Think Tank," said Patti.

"Or a cerebellows," Harrumphrey harrumphed.

"Um . . . don't take this the wrong way," said Leslie. "But maybe you guys just aren't very good at building weapons." She pointed to the Fright Bulb and Flying Pan, lying idle on a nearby table.

The professor nodded. "The laboratories of creaturedom are places of *creation*. Never destruction."

"Except when Reggie starts singing, you mean," said Bildorf.

Pib snickered, and Reggie responded with a shake of his head, using his tusks to knock the two hobmongrels off his shoulders. They clung to his chest of medals and, a moment later, climbed back up in silence.

"The professor might be right," said Harrumphrey. "We'd be better off presenting one of Elliot and Leslie's Onion Stunners or Fluffy Pillow Pitchers than anything *we* came up with."

"That's it!" said Elliot. "Harrumphrey, you *really are* a genius!"

"It's true, but I still don't know what you're talking about."

Elliot smiled proudly. "What if Leslie and I came up with something?"

"*Us?*" asked Leslie.

"Sure! If we came up with an idea, it would give the creatures time to practice."

Professor von Doppler regarded Leslie and his nephew with

more than a little skepticism. "You two really think you can come up with something that will set Gügor free?"

"We already proved we could invent anti-ghork devices," said Elliot. "They're sort of like weapons."

"And they might have worked perfectly," said Leslie, "if we hadn't run out of cheese and onions so quickly."

The professor considered the suggestion for a moment. His expression hardened, as if realizing he had no other choice. He placed a reassuring hand on Elliot and Leslie's shoulders. "Get to it, you two. We'll start rehearsing."

The creatures cleared away a section of the dungeon laboratory and began running through their lines. They wrote new parts for the Heppleworth creatures, while Leslie and Elliot tried to think of something that would impress the bloodthirsty Chief of Quazicom.

"What if," said Elliot, "we combined all of our anti-ghork devices into one gigantic superweapon?"

Leslie wasn't sure that was such a good idea. "How would we fit them all together? And what in the world would we call it?"

Elliot considered this. "Something like a Stinky . . . Funky . . . Fluffy . . . Four-Stringed . . . Onion-Scented . . . Slobber Gun."

The words hung in the air for a moment, and then—

Elliot and Leslie burst out laughing. It was such a ridiculous thing to say, they couldn't help it. They doubled over, helpless with giggles and gasping for breath. In fact, they laughed so hard that over on the far side of the lab, they interrupted the creatures' rehearsal.

"Hmm . . ." said Harrumphrey (who, like the others, had no idea why the two children were laughing). "Maybe we're funnier than we thought."

Finally, Elliot and Leslie caught their breath. When they looked up at each other, they had their "Eureka!" moment.

"That's it!" they said, in perfect unison.

"We can not only make something that'll satisfy the Chief . . ." said Elliot.

". . . but also something that's guaranteed to make Giggles laugh!" said Leslie.

"Which means the Chief will never get to use it!"

"Because we will have *saved the day*!"

Elliot opened his knapsack, took out some paper, and used his original DENKi-3000 Electric Pencil to sketch out a hasty diagram. Leslie watched as a strange device began to take shape. Then she borrowed the pencil herself.

"It's perfect," she said, "but something tells me it'll only work if we get the color right. So how about some hot-pink lightning bolts!" She whisked them across the page.

Elliot laughed. "I can't believe I'm about to say this about hot-pink lightning bolts, but . . . yes! Perfect!"

When they finished the diagram, they brought it over to the other creatures to see. Jean-Remy fluttered up to hover over the page. "Aha! Yes, it is brilliant!" He turned to Elliot, admiringly. "It is clear you have not merely transformed into a creature *on the outside*." He tapped a tiny finger to his temple. "You have *ze brain* of a creature, as well! You too, Leslie, have ze same special gift—even if you're not quite as hairy."

"Fine by me," said Leslie.

"The cabaret begins soon," said the professor. "We'll have to get a prototype rickem-ruckemed together as quick as we can. If only we had Gügor to help us!"

"Don't you worry, Doc," said Cosmo Clutch. "You might

be surprised to know I'm a dab hand at a bit of rickem-ruckery myself."

"You are?" asked Patti.

"Sure," replied the danger-moose. He sliced the air with a flurry of karate chops. "Rickem-ruckery's all about fearlessly fighting with an angry machine, right?"

Harrumphrey winced. "In a manner of speaking . . ."

"Stellar! Then I'm your moose. Nobody's as fearless as I am." As if to prove it, Cosmo snatched up the diagram Elliot and Leslie had drawn. "You all keep rehearsing and leave it to Old Clutchie!" He sauntered over to a pile of a equipment and began kicking at it with the toe of his boot.

"Are you sure he knows what he's doing?" Leslie asked.

"Indubitably!" said Reggie. "I'd trust that danger-moose with my life." Reggie leaned down and whispered to Leslie, "You ought to know, he holds two world records in wild dish-washer wrangling."

"Is that even a thing?" asked Elliot.

Reggie smiled. "It is where *he* comes from."

"Wait!" said Leslie suddenly. "Hold everything. Is it just me, or is everyone forgetting something?"

"Forgetting what?" asked Patti.

"If we're making a brand-new invention, how do we power it? That's the most important thing. Where do we get *the essences*?"

"Where else?" said the professor. "From the Abstractory."

CHAPTER 24

In which Elliot and Leslie meet a new keeper

Elliot and Leslie could hardly believe it, but it was true:
The dungeons came with their very own Abstractory!

"Keep in mind," said the professor, leading Elliot
and Leslie through several lonely caverns, "before the ghorks
turned all this into a dungeon, it was part of the Heppleworth
Creature Department, including what every good creature
department can't do without—an Abstractory!"

They had arrived at a set of double doors, built in the shape
of an Erlenmeyer flask. The professor knocked twice, and with
a crackling hiss, the doors rumbled open of their own accord.

Inside, the Heppleworth Abstractory looked much like the
one at DENKi-3000, where Lester, Chester, and Nestor Preston
tended to the multitude of essences that powered creaturely
inventions. As soon as they entered, they were greeted by a jungle of bookcase-trees, arranged in a winding labyrinth of shelves
and stacks. Unlike the Preston Brothers' abstractory, however,
many of these shelves were empty.

Facing the entrance, seated at a shabby desk, was a creature
unlike anything Elliot and Leslie had met before. It was covered

in bright pink hair and had the rippling physique of a professional wrestler, with broad shoulders that went straight across from right to left, seemingly without a head in between. Instead, there were only three unblinking eyes, each one the size of a perfectly ripe grapefruit. They rose up on three fluffy pink stalks from the creature's shoulders (the right one the lowest, the left slightly higher, and the middle one highest of all). Directly below these glossy orbs, smack in the middle of the creature's chest, was a huge mouth, framed by ruby-red lips and filled with softly rounded teeth.

In spite of the creature's formidable stockiness, there was something distinctly feminine about its shape.

"Whatever you're looking for, don't bother," said the creature. "We're all out." She had the shrill voice of an old-time schoolmarm.

"Elliot, Leslie," said the professor. "This is Orphelina Trunkbasket, keeper of the Heppleworth Abstractory. She and I have known each other for a long time. Nearly everything I know about applied abstraction I learned from her. Orphelina, I'd like you to meet my nephew, Elliot, and his friend Leslie."

For the first time, Orphelina blinked. Three sets of long pink lashes flickered up and down. "Peachy to meet you," she said. Then, one by one, all three of her eyes settled on Elliot. "Your uncle Archimedes was the first human critter I ever taught." She leaned across her desk. "I don't admit it much, but he was one of my best students." The stalk of her middle eyeball tilted forward until it was inches from Elliot's face. "Which leaves me wondering . . . are you as good at choosing essences as he is?"

Before Elliot could answer, Leslie spoke up. "You have three eyes. And back at DENKi-3000, the Preston brothers have three heads. I can't help thinking that's not a coincidence."

Orphelina's attention whipped over to Leslie. "Well, girlie, you certainly have an *eye* for detail." Her left eye winked. "I like that! And you're absolutely right. When it comes to Abstractory keepers, three's the magic number. Every creature invention requires *three essences*, so we keepers reflect that. Three heads, three arms, three stomachs—you get the picture. In my case, I got a trio of peepers. Pretty standard stuff to see at an abstractory, but . . ." Orphelina paused. All three of her eyes narrowed. "Bah! *What* abstractory? All they left me was fumes and fizzle! There's no point even going in!"

"Please, Orphelina, let the children have a look around. They've had an idea for a very important invention, and it's going to need the proper essences." He took a deep breath and placed his hands on Elliot and Leslie's shoulders. "I'll think you'll find these two are even better at choosing them than I am."

Orphelina squinted at the children. "Hard to believe, but I'll see what I can do."

"Thank you," said the professor. "I've got to get back to rehearsal." He turned and hastened back toward the laboratory portion of the dungeon.

When the professor was gone, Orphelina placed her fuzzy pink hands flat on her desk. "Listen, kids, I wish I could help you, but I can't."

Leslie was shocked. "But you just said—"

"*I know* what I just said, but I was just trying to get rid of your boss."

"He's not our boss," said Elliott. "He's my uncle."

"Either way, this whole place is kaput! Sold out! Sapped dry! Read my lips: *There. Is. Nothing. Left.*"

"Sure there is," said Leslie. "You have tons of essences left."

She pointed to the countless shelves behind the desk. Although many of them were bare, quite a few others trembled and flashed with just the sort of outlandish substances they expected to find in an abstractory.

"Nothing but duds," said Orphelina.

"Maybe we should have a look for ourselves." Elliot moved to step around the desk, but Orphelina stood up, raising an arm to block his way. "Oy! Weren't you listening?" She grabbed the scruff of Elliot's knapsack and lifted him off his feet.

"You know something," said Elliot, "for an abstractory keeper, you're not very helpful."

"Listen, you—*and you!*" She pointed at Leslie. "I'm not having *one squidge* of my essences used to power a single spring, transistor, or even the teeniest, weeniest cog in the sort of invention you two want to make!"

Elliot craned his head closer to Orphelina's trio of eyes. "But we haven't even told you what we're making."

"*Weapons!*" said Orphelina. "Isn't that right? For Quazicom, no less! Well, you can forget about it. It's not happening."

"But we're not making a weapon," said Leslie. "Well, not a weapon like the Chief wants. It's not something that will hurt people."

"It'll do the exact opposite," said Elliot. He lowered his voice and whispered the name of their invention.

"Intriguing," said Orphelina. She lowered Elliot to the floor. "I suppose I could let you have a look around, but I'm sorry to say that when I told you I've got nothing but duds in here, I wasn't kidding. When Quazicom took over, they shipped out all my best essences, and left me with only the negatives."

"Negatives?" Leslie asked.

"Negative essences. Fear, Disgruntlement, Jealousy. The essence of Stepping in a Warm Puddle of Slobberwolf Vomit. That sort of thing. When offset by a positive essence, you can achieve a kind of harmony. For instance, you put a few shards of Anger in with a dollop of Apology, and you might be able to invent something to strengthen emotional bonds between siblings. But just the Anger?" Orphelina shook her head. "With nothing but negative essences, all you can really make are weapons. That's why the Chief cleared out all the good ones."

"Negative essences," Leslie whispered. She was curious. What would that mean? She descended the entranceway steps down to the nearest bookcase-tree. The first vessel she saw was a simple glass jar full of a viscous slate-gray sludge like wet cement. The surface bubbled and popped in a slow boil, and the moment Leslie fixed her eyes on it, its color shifted from dour gray to a murky purple, and then a pale, lifeless yellow. The colors kept changing, each one a sallow, half-hearted version of a brighter hue, but when Leslie looked away, the sludge returned to gray. The label on the jar said:

Mendacity

"Lying," Orphelina explained. She and Elliot had come down to join Leslie. The three of them stood around the trunk of the first bookcase-tree. "That's what mendacity means, to be dishonest."

"Bad essences," Leslie whispered, beginning to understand.

"Look at this one." Elliot reached his hairy paw into the shelf and pulled out a plump blue bottle. Clinging to the inside of the jar was a finely spun cobweb. Suspended at its center was a throbbing black heart, while all across the web, tiny spiders scuttled back and forth. When one of them ventured too close to the throbbing heart, it was instantly sucked inside, and for a brief moment the heart beat faster.

Elliot shuddered as he watched several of the spiders consumed, and yet there were always more appearing out of nowhere, ready to feed the hungry muscle at the center of its web. On the side of this jar it said:

Selfishness

"You see," Orphelina lamented. "This is all they've left me."

"There has to be *something* in here we can use," said Leslie. "If there's one thing I've learned about creature physics, it's that it always surprises you with hidden alcoves and secret passages." Leslie stepped past the first bookcase-tree and into a landscape like a diseased forest, a once lush jungle stripped to only the barest leaves and blossoms. "Come on, Elliot, I'll bet we can find something. This is what we're good at, remember?"

Elliot followed his friend, recalling the Preston Brothers' advice. "We just have to let our feet wander through the shelves," he said, "and let our minds wander, too."

So they did, but Orphelina was right. On shelves that should have brimmed with essences, they found only dust, while the jars and bottles they did discover contained essences that were useless to them: Revulsion (a jar of slimy bile), Glibness (a bottle writhing with slippery pink tongues), Chaos (a container floating with the ruined remains of smashed dollhouse furniture), or Procrastination (an old reliquary full of handless watch faces).

With the hour of the cabaret fast approaching, they decided

to split up in hopes of covering more ground. They soon found that, as with DENKi-3000's Abstractory, the deeper they went, the more peculiar (and more *creaturely*) the essences became. Leslie found the Lingering Sense of Defeat after Arm Wrestling a Marrowrangler (a bottle of shadowy rain clouds), and the Idleness of a Slumber-Sloth (a lump of cold stone, shaggy with moss). Meanwhile, Elliot came upon the Cowardice of a Jellyboned Wimplebeest (a jar of yellow custard), and the Anxiety of Not Knowing Where to Look While Having Tea with a Many-Eyed Goggle-Ogler (a jar of cloudy fluid, floating with—what else?—*eyeballs*).

"Elliot! Over here!"

Exactly as Leslie predicted, there was a hidden room the ghorks had missed. The entrance was concealed at the end of one of the narrowest isles.

"I just let my mind wander," Leslie told Elliot when he joined her. "My eyes went a bit fuzzy, and then I saw it—a secret door!"

It was perfectly round, with a hollow knot in the wood. When Leslie poked her finger into the knot, Elliot heard a click, and the door came open. They crawled through and found a small dark room. As soon as they entered they knew they had found what they had hoped to find. The room fluttered with lus-ter bugs and *brimmed with essences*!

"You found it!" Elliot was so happy he couldn't help but give Leslie a hug.

She was less than receptive. "Quit it, you're like a porcupine!"

Elliot jumped back. He had forgotten about his transforma-tion into a three-toed bristle-imp. Perhaps it was a sign he was growing more comfortable in his creaturely skin. It was just as

Jean-Remy said. He had become a creature—inside and out. But he couldn't think about that now. They had work to do, *finding the right essences.* "We need to find the three funniest, silliest ones they have," he told Leslie.

He had only just turned to begin the search when she answered, "What about this one?"

It was a cylindrical jar of subtly frosted glass. Inside, a ring of misty figures stood shoulder to shoulder, all of them facing outward.

"Is it just me," Leslie asked, "or do these guys all look like Reggie?"

Elliot squinted into the glass. "They're bombastadons."

At first glance, the figures looked like ghosts, made of nothing but mist. But a closer look revealed they were actually composed of falling snow, tiny flakes that fluttered down to collect on their feet, which were the whitest, most substantial part of their bodies. Each of the ghostly bombastadons raised their knees and kicked out their toes in perfect unison, like a bizarre cross between marching soldiers and dancing girls. The label said:

The Closing Ceremonies of a Bombastadon's Midwinter Boot-Washing Festival

Elliot laughed. "It's perfect!"

He slipped the jar into his knapsack and cradled the glass with the fabric of his fishing vest. His fishing vest. He had never gone for so long without it before.

They moved through the small array of shelves, until an oddly shaped bottle caught Elliot's eye. It had a spiraling, conical shape like a seashell, and it was full of what appeared to be *throat loz-enges*. Each one had been painted with a cartoonish drawing of a face, its mouth wide open and its tongue lolling comically out from one side. The label said:

A Screaming Wee-Beast Discovers Laryngitis

Leslie giggled. "Yep, that one's silly enough!"

It was Leslie again who found the third and final essence. It was a multicolored stained-glass jar with a tiny disco ball hanging down inside it. At the bottom, short lengths of colorful yarn had knotted themselves into shapes that Leslie recognized as creatures, and all of them were doing an absurd rendition of a disco dance. The Hustle, the Robot, the Bump, the Boogaloo, the Penguin—they were doing them all!

"Here's number three," Leslie said, passing the bottle to Elliot. He laughed when he read the label, which said:

Hitting the Disco with a Dandemalion Schboov

"Perfect," he said, but when he peered into the jar, his laughter stopped. He saw something inside he didn't expect to see: *himself.* A hundred tiny images of Elliot's face flashed in the mirrored squares of the spinning disco ball. He saw, at last, what he looked like.

In the countless reflections, he saw a face completely covered in the same moss-green hair that covered the rest of his body. He saw a canine snout, softly shining teeth, and a thin pink tongue. He saw pointed tufts of hair hanging from his cheeks and a pair of broad fox-like ears rising from the top of his head. The only part of his face he recognized were his eyes, blinking back at him from behind a pair of crooked glasses. He straightened them.

I really am *the world's dorkiest werewolf,* he thought.

As he looked at himself, Elliot felt a strange calmness come over him. It was as if he was gazing upon his true form. Hadn't he been obsessed with creaturedom ever since he had discovered it? Wasn't it true that, more than anything else in the world, he wanted only to be like his uncle, deep in the world of creatures? And what about when he shouted at his parents at that restaurant? He had done that because of how different he felt from them. A different . . . *species.*

"It's the real me," he whispered. *"I am a creature."*

"I know that," said Leslie. "You've been one since this morning! But we can't just stand around admiring ourselves in tiny disco balls! The cabaret'll be starting soon! We have to go!"

After thanking Orphelina, they carried their essences back to the laboratory. Harrumphrey, Patti, Jean-Remy, and the other creatures were crowded around a table, its top covered with a white silk cloth. An odd shape, the size of a lumpy watermelon, lay beneath it.

"We banged this together as fast as we could, but it should work—provided you've brought us the right essences."

"Can we see it?" Elliot reached for the white cloth, but Harrumphrey stepped forward to block his way.

"Not so fast," grumbled the hufflehead. "Before you can see the prototype, you have to promise us something."

Elliot's hairy green face rumpled suspiciously. "Should I be scared right now?"

Patti folded her arms sternly. "Since it was your bright idea to have us perform in this crazy food festival cabaret, we've decided it's only right if *you* perform, too."

"*Me?!*"

Leslie laughed. "Looking like that, you'll fit right in!"

"So will you," said Patti, looking at Leslie.

Leslie pointed to herself in surprise. "But *I'm* not a creature."

"Neither am I," said the professor, "but we've all got to do our part. If we're going to save the day with cabaret, we'll need everyone's help."

Bildorf and Pib, perched as ever atop Reggie's epaulets, shimmied their hips and sang, "Save the day with *ca-ba-ret*! Save the day with *ca-ba-ret*!"

"Save it for the song-and-dance number, you two!" Elliot flapped his arms for them to stop chanting the silly slogan. "All right, we'll do it," he told his uncle. "We'll perform. So *now* can we see our—"

"That's it!" cried Cosmo Clutch, who until then had been standing alone by the wall, sucking thoughtfully on his chocolate cigar. "I knew there was something!"

"What are you talking about?" asked Leslie.

Cosmo rushed over. "That's it! That's the answer! *Cabaret!*" He grabbed the professor's shoulders and shook him like a human maraca. "*That's* the only thing that can save a Wednesday!"

Everyone stared at Cosmo Clutch.

"Aren't you excited?" asked the daredevil, squinting at his friends. "With cabaret we can't fail!"

"I hate to burst your bubble," said Leslie, "but today's Saturday."

Cosmo slapped his forehead. His antlers trembled with disappointment. "One of these days I'm going to invest in a calendar."

The professor looked down at the lumpy sheet on the table. "It's a good thing we've got a backup plan."

"Speaking of which . . ." Elliot looked to Jean-Remy. "Can we *please* see our invention now?"

Jean-Remy swooped up to the table and whipped away the cloth. Underneath was what appeared to be a set of bagpipes, but with one pipe larger than the rest. The larger one resembled the barrel of a bazooka or a blunderbuss, with one significant difference. Extending out from the end of the barrel was a creaturely hand, complete with fuzzy brown hair and cartoonish yellow claws. The fingers of the hand hung slack, as if it had been trying to make a fist but had given up mid-clutch. As if it was straining toward the very last cookie at the bottom of a very deep cookie jar. Zigzagging across the device were a series of comical pink lightning bolts. The overall effect was one of utter ridiculousness.

Elliot and Leslie smiled at each other.

"It's perfect!" they cried.

CHAPTER 25

In which the audience thinks it's all part of the show

If you had been in the Simmersville market square that warm Saturday evening, you would have been in for quite a show. The stalls and restaurants around the edge of the square teemed with people. You might have noticed one stall was more popular than all the others, a stall clouded in a perpetual puff of steam. Deep inside the mist, a woman with long black hair passed out small cardboard boxes filled with delicious dumplings.

Despite the popularity of the stall, it was clear the woman was worried. Her anxious eyes looked past every customer she served, searching the crowd for something, or perhaps *someone*. The woman, of course, was Leslie's mother. Imagine how surprised she would have been to learn that, at that very moment, her daughter was right below her feet. . . .

Leslie, Professor von Doppler, the creatures of DENKi-3000, Cosmo Clutch, Elliot, and the other "specimens" were all being ushered along a huge tunnel directly below the Simmersville market square. Leading the way were the Five Ghorks. Behind them came the charred black palanquin that contained Giggles, the Fabled Sixth Ghork. Last in the procession was the monstrous blender, with Gügor, Eloise-Yvette, and Dr. Benedict Heppleworth, still locked in a cage, dangling helplessly above its glittering blades.

Gügor still lay motionless on the floor of the cage, with Eloise-Yvette still hovering above his face, softly singing to him. Dr. Heppleworth stood near the bars. If he was angry or resentful or even frightened, his face showed nothing but an eerie calm. Nevertheless, he must have known that if Elliot and Leslie's plan failed, all three of them would be gobbled by ghorks.

They emerged from a hidden exit into an alleyway adjacent to the stage. They saw the market square was packed with people; it was standing room only for the famous cabaret.

On the stage, three women—a juggler, a contortionist, and a fire-eater—were all dressed up like peacocks. Elliot wondered if, with all that plumage, eating fire was such a good idea. But when their performance reached its climax (featuring a chainsaw, a pyrotechnic rubber chicken, three bowling balls, and a whole circus of somersaults), all three women emerged unscathed.

The crowd cheered. On the huge view-screen above the stage, the cabaret emcee appeared. He was a plump-faced man with rosy cheeks and a smile like he was trying to sell you a barbecue on late-night television.

"Wonderful! Amazing! Stupendous!" he cried. "Wasn't that just *magnificent*?"

The crowd clapped politely, and the image of the emcee's face trembled and vanished from the view-screen. A moment later, the man himself sauntered onstage. His body was as plump as his face, and he wore a gleaming white suit to match his shimmering teeth. Under his arm he carried a clipboard, clamped with white paper.

"Now, tell me," he called to the crowd, "how many people

here like . . ."—he flipped a page on his clipboard—"*The Plaice to Be* fish and chip shop?"

"*HOOORAY!*" shouted the crowd.

"And what about our *Kebabylon Nights* Turkish restaurant?"

"*HOOORAY!*"

"I'm sure many of you have already sampled the delectable sirloin steaks at *The Grill from Ipanema*!"

"*HOOORAY!*"

The emcee rattled off a list of Simmersville's silliest restaurants.

"*Thai-ranysaurus Rex!*"

"*Balti Towers!*"

"*The Pie's the Limit!*"

"*HOOORAY! HOOORAY! HOOORAY!*"

"Well then, you're all in for a treat," the emcee went on, "because after our next performance, we'll be serving the food festival's Final Feast, featuring the best food from all these and more!"

The promise of one last meal received the loudest cheer of all. Then, while the emcee went on with more of his patter, technicians cleared the stage and set up a drum kit, microphones, and keyboards for the next performance. Seeing this, Leslie grabbed Elliot's hairy arm and squeezed.

"*Ow!*"

"This is it!" Leslie whispered. "They're on next!"

Elliot was confused. "*Who's* on next?"

"You know, *them*!"

"Now," said the emcee, "what everyone's been waiting for! Ladies and gentlemen, it is my sincere pleasure to introduce those costumed, capering crooners . . . *Boris Minor and the Karloffs*!"

The crowd went wild. Leslie went wild, too, jumping up and

down and squeezing Elliot's arm so fiercely his fingers tingled. "*Stop that!*"

First, the drummer came onstage, in his usual outlandish getup. The crowd gasped because his costume was so strange and yet so lifelike. He resembled a four-armed hammerhead shark. When he took his seat at the drum kit, he picked up not two, not three, but *four* drumsticks. Then came the lead guitarist, a horned, bright-red she-demon; the bass player, whose thick mop of blond hair grew all the way down to his feet, hiding his entire body save for his two spindly gray arms (with which he held his instrument); and the keyboardist, who resembled a portly lemon-colored tree sloth in a black trilby and matching bow tie.

Finally, clomping onstage with a slow, zombie-like shuffle was Boris Minor himself. His face and neck were an ugly patchwork of scars and stitches, and the bolts on the sides of his neck spurted steam with every step. His voice, however, was as smooth and sweet as a pot of honey.

"Simmersville," he purred into the microphone. "Are you ready to rock?"

"*YEEEAAH!*"

KER-RANG! With a deep reverberating twang from the hairy bass-player's guitar, the band launched into one of their biggest hits, "The Zombie Stomp":

Let's d-d-do the monster bash!
Those feet, you stamp.
That head, you thrash.
Those hips, you shake.
Those teeth, you gnash.
Do it, baby . . . with m-m-much panache!

Now t-t-try the zombie stomp!

Put out your arms.

Go clump and clomp!

On stiff old legs

Go tramp and tromp!

Let's find some brains . . . to ch-ch-champ and chomp!

Now how 'bout the creature conga!

You know the words

So sing along-gah!

You feel the beat?

So bang your gong-gah!

Do whatcha like! Ain't n-n-nothin' wron-gah!

"*BLEGH!*" said Wingnut. "There's nothing I hate more than gothic surf-rock!" He grabbed two of Digits's enormous fingertips and shoved them in his ears.

Up on stage, the view-screen above the band flickered and fizzled. The vague silhouette of a man appeared. It was the Chief!

"There he is," said Grinner, leading the prisoners toward the square. "Get movin', creeps."

Boris Minor and the Karloffs were just reaching the end of the song when the marching procession of ghorks, the creatures of DENKi-3000, the palanquin, and the gigantic electric blender all emerged from the alleyway. At first, the crowd was so enthralled with the music, they barely noticed. In fact, quite a few people in the crowd waved to the ghorks, believing the appearance of a bunch of ogres (or trolls or perhaps overgrown gremlins) was all part of the show.

Even when the ghorks threw an enormous net over the entire stage, the crowd cheered at the sudden heightening of drama. The only ones put off by the arrival of the ghorks were the band itself.

"What's the deal?" Boris Minor droned into his mic, never once losing his incredible cool, even as the ropes of netting tangled around his skeletal body. "In case you hadn't noticed, we're trying to play a gig here."

The ghorks didn't care. They yanked the band offstage in a cacophony of feedback and sour notes. Boris Minor and his bandmates were promptly hoisted up, instruments and all, and slung from a nearby building's fire escape.

"My sincerest apologies to the entertainment," said the Chief (in a voice that wasn't apologetic at all), "but there's been a change of plans."

"That's odd." The emcee flipped frantically through the pages on his clipboard. "I don't remember anyone else on the bill."

"Good people of Simmersville," said the Chief, "I'm sure you'll be happy to know the guest of honor has finally arrived."

The palanquin was carried on stage and set down in the corner. The door was opened, and from inside, the ghork attendants brought out a throne. It was jaggedly carved from the same black wood as the palanquin itself. Then Giggles emerged, his face as imperiously blank as ever.

"Now," said the Chief, "I'd like to introduce the *real* final performance of the evening. I've been told it's guaranteed to make everyone here laugh. *Everyone.*" His shadowy eyes glared down at Giggles. "Let's see if that's true."

Elliot, Leslie, and their friends were pushed up onto the stage. Leslie took the opportunity to wave to her mother, hoping to let her know she was okay, but instead of looking relieved to have finally found her daughter, Mrs. Fang folded her arms and glared at the professor and his creatures. Elliot saw his own parents standing near the entrance to the Simmersville Inn. When he waved to them, they didn't respond. Of course they didn't. How could they know the hairy green bristle-imp on stage was really their son?

"*Oooh!* I get it!" said a man in the front row. "*Creatures!*" He pointed to Boris Minor and the band, to the ghorks flanking the stage, and finally to the creatures of DENKi-3000. "That must be the theme for this year's cabaret."

"I'm not really into fantasy," said the woman beside him, "but you have to hand it to the organizers. Those costumes are *unbelievable!*"

"Somebody wanna explain," droned Boris Minor, still dangling inside the net, "what the green dudes are doing on the stage? 'Cuz, y'see, no offense, but I thought *we* were the big finale." He sighed heavily. "Could somebody get our booking agent on the phone?"

Professor von Doppler trembled to the front of the stage. Stooping over the microphone, he looked crooked and uncomfortable. It was clear he was incredibly nervous. "M-Mr. M-M-Minor, sir? We're t-terribly sorry for interrupting your p-p-performance, but there's been . . ." He gulped, and the *plonking* sound of his Adam's apple echoed from every speaker. "There's b-b-been an unfortunate change of p-plans. So without f-further ado, I w-would like to introduce, in their t-triumphant d-d-debut here at the Simmersville F-F-F-F-Food Festival D-Dinner-Theatre-Style Cabaret, the curious, delirious, *hilarious* creatures of DENKi-3000!"

MAGNETIC BELT

3000

CHAPTER 26

In which Cosmo Clutch does some fancy footwork,
Reggie smashes the footlights, and the Chief would
have preferred a death ray

here is a special brand of joy that comes from discovering creatures are real. It is a joy that makes you feel lighter than air, as if you are floating away from all of life's worries, bouncing on a soft pink cloud of pure giddiness. That warm Saturday evening, the audience in the Simmersville market square laughed with just this sort of joy.

Or, to put it another way, they laughed and laughed *and laughed*! The performance from the creatures was filled with the strangest music, the most absurd lyrics, and the clumsiest dancing anyone had ever seen. For the creatures themselves, however, there was a problem.

"Look at Giggles," said Leslie. She was standing in the back row of performers, waving jazz hands and doing awkward, bow-legged knee bends with everyone else. "He hasn't even twitched."

"Just wait," Elliot told her. "The show's not over yet."

Cosmo Clutch had taken Gügor's place in the performance. He compensated for his tone deafness with fearlessly fancy footwork. When he attempted the splits, he pulled a rather tender muscle—and the crowd roared with laughter. (Not Giggles, though. He didn't react at all.)

At last, it was time for the newest additions to the performance: Elliot and Leslie. They fist pumped and knee bended to the front of the stage, while the creatures performed a poorly choreographed interpretive dance, meant to reflect their emotions (it didn't).

Leslie went first:

> My name's Leslie. Here's my tale.
> Is it weird? It's off the scale!
> In the park is where it started.
> I was feeling sour-hearted!

> Glum and sitting on a bench,
> pretending I was (sort of) French.
> Then my friend here came along
> and showed me where I might belong!

> Now my crew is kind of freaky,
> *very* weird (and *very* geeky).
> But friends like them? They're not so bad.
> They're the best I've ever had!

And so on.

The crowd laughed and cheered for Leslie's verses, but Giggles remained unmoved. Then it was Elliot's turn:

> Hi there, folks, I'm Ell-i-ot!
> I'm giving cabaret a shot!

First of all, I have to say
I'm not supposed to look this way!

These teeth? These claws? All this hair?
(I have it growing *everywhere*!)
I'm now a creature, to the core,
I'll be this way . . . forevermore!

So listen, Mom! And listen, Dad!
I'm sorry if I made you mad.
I hollered at you both this morning.
I ran away, without a warning.

So please accept, to you, from me,
this musical apology!
I'm still your kid, your only one,
your hairy creature of a son!

A fuzzy, slightly dorky shrimp
(specifically, a 'bristle-imp').
Furry! Itchy! Prickly! Starchy!
But please—don't be mad at Uncle Archie.

I'm just a fuzzball, that's my fate.
I think it was . . . *something I ate*!
So Simmersville, your food is nice,
but skip 'the Special'—that's my advice!

Finally, looking once again to thump into the spotlight at the very last moment, Reggie thundered forward. Bildorf and Pib gripped tenaciously to his epaulettes in a clumsy trio. First, there was Bildorf:

> Well, we hope you liked our dance,
> And laughed so hard you wet your pants!

Then Pib:

> But now's the end, and so we say
> We hope you liked our cabaret!

At last, all together, Reggie, Bildorf, and Pib sang out: "O U U U U R R R R R   C A A A A A A - B A A A A A A A - R E E E E E E E E E E E E T !"

Reggie sang the last syllable, and his submaritone shattered every one of the footlights. The crowd was about to rise to their feet for a standing ovation, only they couldn't. They were laughing too hard. The song and dance of the creature cabaret had been so absurd, the crowd was incapacitated with laughter.

Unfortunately, the only reaction from Giggles was a single yawn.

Elliot hung his head. It hadn't worked. Giggles hadn't so much as tittered. The cabaret had failed. Up on the view-screen, even the Chief seemed a bit disappointed.

"I suppose," he said to himself, "a fiendishly dry sense of humor is the best the ghorks have got." He shook his head, as if being let down by his mottled green henchmen was an experience he had all too often. "*Figures*," he muttered, shrugging his shadowy shoulders. "At least I've got a gigantic blender to cheer me up."

The Chief snapped his fingers, and one of the hand-ghorks rushed eagerly to the blender's controls. He pressed one enormous button labeled *Purée*.

WHIZZZZZZZ! went the blender's countless blades.

"*Ooooh!*" went the audience, who could hardly believe there was more excitement to come. Now they assumed they were being treated to a Houdini-style escape routine. In the top corner of the view-screen, a timer appeared. It showed five minutes on the clock—and it began to count down.

(*4:59 . . .*)

Inside the cage, Eloise-Yvette slapped Gügor's face and tugged on his colorful dreadlocks. "Wake up, Googy!" she cried. "You are the only one strong enough to break us out of here—*I hope*! But please! You must wake up!"

(*4:55 . . .*)

Even Dr. Heppleworth, who had been so stoic until now, leapt around Gügor, trying to shake him awake. But Gügor didn't move.

"Wait! Stop!" said Elliot, waving his hand at the view-screen. "You can't do this!"

"Elliot's right," cried Leslie, "you said you'd only grind them up if we failed to give you a special DENKi-3000 superweapon!"

"I know," said the Chief, "and you haven't."

"But we have it right here!" said Elliot.

The Chief seemed surprised. "Really? Where?"

(*4:39 . . .*)

Leslie ran to the professor. All along, he had been hiding the device under his lab coat (this was partly why he seemed so awkward at the microphone, and why his posture had been so crooked and lumpy). From under his lab coat, Leslie pulled the strange bagpipe-bazooka, covered with flamingo-pink lightning bolts.

"*That?*" asked the Chief. "*That's* the DENKi-3000 Creature Department's idea of an ultimate weapon?!"

"What's the matter with it?" asked Elliot.

The Chief frowned. "It looks like a . . . like a . . . well, I don't know what it looks like, but it certainly doesn't look very menacing."

"Even so," said Elliot, "I'll bet you're dying to know what it is."

"Maybe. . . ." said the Chief.

"Admit it," said Leslie.

"Fine! I admit it! Just tell me already!"

"You told us you wanted a revolutionary weapon," Elliot said. "Well, there's nothing more revolutionary than this!" He pointed to the strange device in Leslie's arms.

"We call it," said Leslie, "*the Tickle-Fingler!*"

"Excuse me?" said the Chief.

"The Tickle-Fingler," Elliot repeated.

"Please," begged the Chief, "tell me that's secret code for 'apocalyptic death-ray.'"

(*4:04 . . .*)

"It's kind of the opposite of an apocalyptic death-ray," said Elliot.

Up on the view-screen, the Chief threw up his hands. "How can an ultimate weapon be *the opposite* of an apocalyptic death-ray?! An apocalyptic death-ray *is* an ultimate weapon. It's the *ultimate* ultimate weapon, everybody knows that!"

Elliot smiled. "This is even better."

"Is it at least a maiming ray?" asked the Chief hopefully.

Leslie shook her head. "Sorry."

"Does it draw blood?"

"Never."

The Chief threw up his hands. "What's left?! A poke-in-the-eye ray?"

"Nope," said Elliot. "The Tickle-Fingler shoots a one hundred percent *giggle-beam*!"

"A laser of pure silliness," Leslie explained.

"And *that's* what makes it so revolutionary," Elliot went on. "What you're looking at is a totally effective weapon, one that leaves whoever you use it on completely helpless, but it comes with *no apocalypse required*!"

Leslie grinned proudly. "No one even gets poked in the eye."

(*3:32* . . .)

The Chief made a gravelly grumbling noise from the back of his throat. "So when you say effective, in a more accurate way, you mean *in*effective."

"Nope! Watch this." Leslie pulled the Tickle-Fingler's trigger and squeezed its air bladder under her armpit. Instantly, the fingers on the end of the bazooka barrel started wriggling like worms. There was a loud electrostatic *crack,* and a spiraling beam of purple light shot from the fingers. Leslie waved the giggle-beam over the crowd, and every person in the audience started laughing, even harder than they had at the cabaret. These weren't regular, run-of-the-mill, knock-knock-joke guffaws. These were deep, all-encompassing, *all-consuming* hysterics. In moments, every face in the crowd had turned red and glistened with sweat. People were doubled over, clutching their guts and choking on their own mirth.

"Perhaps," said the Chief, "I was wrong about the Tickle-Fingler."

(3:05 . . .)

"Wait," said Elliot, "there's one more thing. We're going to show you how wrong you were about Giggles—by finally making him laugh!"

Leslie swung the Tickle-Fingler around and aimed its beam at the Fabled Sixth Ghork. It struck Giggles right between the eyes, but had no effect. Giggles merely went crossed-eyed.

He *still* wasn't laughing.

"What is it with this guy?" Leslie wondered. She squeezed the Tickle-Fingler's air-bladder up to full power. The giggle-beam made the Sixth Ghork's whole body glow a neon purple. Then something very strange happened. His enormous shoes started to laugh. The bulbous toes rose up off the soles and started chuckling.

"*Whoa*," said Elliot. "This thing even works on his shoes!"

"All right," said the Chief. "That's enough. You had your chance, and you failed. But I thank you. I'm beginning to believe what Grinner told me. His dry sense of humor is *so* dry it's tantamount to evil, and you know how the saying goes: *Evil is good!*"

"No, it's not," said Leslie. "You can sort of tell from the word. *Evil*. See?"

"Don't go philosophical on me, kid. I'm a businessman."

The Chief nodded to his henchmen, and the ghorks threw a second net over the stage and trapped the creatures of DENKi-3000. Only Elliot and Leslie, standing at the front of the stage, remained free. But they were soon surrounded by the Five Ghorks.

Leslie spun the Tickle-Fingler to defend them, but Grinner snatched it away from her. He tossed it across the stage, where its air bladder wheezed empty and its wriggling fingers stopped moving. Then Digits snatched up Leslie and Elliot themselves, one each in his huge hands.

"Sorry, kids," said the Chief. "I'm as surprised as you are, but this proves Giggles *really is* who we think he is: the Fabled Sixth Ghork! Anybody *that* joyless gets my vote when it comes to leading a ghork army." The Chief smiled malevolently down on the audience. "So, about that army . . ."

He snapped his fingers, and new processions of ghorks marched out of the alleyways that fed into the market square. All of them were dressed like disheveled waiters and carried domed silver trays, exactly like the one with which Elliot had been served his "Special." The moment Elliot saw them, his heart flipped in his hairy chest. Every one of those dishes would be spiked with the secret potion!

(2:26 . . .)

"No! Stop!" He waved his hairy arms at the crowd. "Remember what I said in my song-and-dance number just now? I said *skip the Special*! I was serious!" Elliot moved his hairy green hand up and down his hairy green body. "Look what it did to me!"

But the crowd only laughed. They still believed it was all part of the show.

"Ladies and gentlemen!" The Chief beamed. "May I proudly present your Simmersville Food Festival Final Feast!"

The ghork waiters lifted the huge domed platters. Under every one was a grotesque dish, each in the shape of a ghork-inspired face. Hideously huge eyes, ears, noses, hands, and mouths all glistened and steamed on the plates.

"No!" cried Leslie. "Please! Don't eat them!"

The festivalgoers just laughed. Many of them were still snickering after being shot with the giggle-beam.

"We've got to stop them," Elliot whispered to Leslie, "but no one believes us."

"Wait," said Leslie. "Remember what you said when you were first served the Special?"

"I don't remember."

(*2:10 . . .*)

"You said, '*If that thing moves, I'm not eating it.*'" Leslie's eyes moved pointedly over to the Tickle-Fingler, lying still on the stage. Elliot immediately understood, but he had to break free of Digits's stifling grip. And there was only one way to do it.

"*RAWR!*"

Elliot snarled like the strange creature he was and sunk his teeth into the flesh of Digits's enormous thumb.

"*Yooooow!* cried Digits, letting go.

Elliot ran for the Tickle-Fingler, picked it up, and kept going, dodging left and right to avoid the grasping hands of the Five Ghorks. Snot-balls from Adenoid Jack's cannon-like nostrils whizzed past his head. Looping the Tickle-Fingler's strap over his shoulder, he inflated the air bladder up to full power. Then he jumped off the stage.

He ran through the crowd, hitting every one of the ghorks' hideous dishes with the giggle-beam. As soon as he did, the dishes began to laugh. Glistening red-pepper lips, chattering corn-on-the-cob teeth, flopping pork-chop tongues, joggling rump-steak cheeks, bulging boiled-egg eyeballs, writhing spaghetti hairdos—it all came to life, cackling maniacally at the diners, who were so terrified they dropped their knives and forks. Their meals weren't just moving . . . *they were laughing*!

(1:42 . . .)

And they *kept* laughing. Elliot's giggle-beam had been so intense, every dish was beginning to disintegrate. The repulsive faces laughed so hard they slid off their platters and dissolved into a runny sludge. In no time, every dish the ghorks had prepared was dripping away between the cracks in the cobblestones.

"You've ruined everything!" cried the Chief.

"Oh, don't worry," replied the emcee. "There's plenty of other dishes we can provide for the Final Feast."

"No!" growled the Chief. "It had to be those ones! We've used up all of the elixir!"

But the chefs from the food stalls didn't mind. They were already coming out with new dishes to replace the ones that had just giggled themselves into oblivion. Frustrated, Grinner jumped off the stage, just as a chef from a nearby food stall was bringing a perfectly cooked filet mignon to one of the diners. He snarled angrily at the man and tipped the chef's plate onto the ground.

"How rude!" The old woman who had been patiently awaiting the steak (which now lay steaming on the cobblestones) picked it up and—*WAP!*—used it to slap Grinner in the face.

Thus began the biggest food fight in the history of Simmersville.

(1:14 . . .)

CHAPTER 27

In which the festivalgoers have a bit of fun

Elliot and Leslie could hardly believe it. It was an astonishing thing to watch. An entire town going head-to-head with an army of ghorks (or ogres, or trolls, or overgrown gremlins, or whatever they were), *and winning.*

Every kind of foodstuff from Simmersville's most famous restaurants flew through the air in a blizzard of fruits and vegetables, meats and cheeses, eggs and flour, herbs and spices, and just about every ingredient you could name.

(0:56 . . .)

The problem facing the ghorks was the same problem Leslie and Elliott had faced all weekend long: No one believed them. Even though everyone in the market square had great globs of snot dripping from their elbows, none of them cared. No one suspected that it was *real.* No one suspected they were smeared with *actual* snot, from *actual* ghorks (who had ever heard of the word "ghork" anyway?). More than anything else, the people of Simmersville were simply having fun, and among the realms of creaturedom, it's common knowledge that *fun* is nearly as powerful as *hope.*

To the ghorks, the power of fun was frightening and offensive. The hands of the hand-ghorks lost their grip; the eyes of the eye-ghorks clouded with bewilderment; the mouths of the mouth-ghorks hung slack in shock; the ears of the ear-ghorks were deafened by the roar of their own dismay; and the noses of the nose-ghorks ran out of boogers.

"Wouldja believe it?" said Leslie. "Regular people taking on the ghorks."

Elliot smiled at her as a boiled turnip sailed past his head. "I have a feeling we're about to save the day."

Leslie was just about to smile back when her face froze. The food-filled pandemonium of the market square had distracted them from something *very* important. Here's a hint as to what it was:

0:41 . . .

"The blender!" cried Elliot.

They spun around and saw the cage that held Gügor, Eloise-Yvette, and Dr. Heppleworth prisoner had been completely swallowed into the mouth of the blender.

Looking down on them from his view-screen, the Chief raised a hand and twiddled his fingers. "You may have foiled my plans for the Final Feast," he rasped, "but I'll still have the distinct pleasure of watching your friends ground to a pulp." He shrugged as if he ground people to a pulp every day. "At least *that's* something I can be proud of."

Through the glass of the blender, the shapes of their friends were as blurry as anything in The Green Fairy restaurant, but they could see the huge orangeish lump that was Gügor, still lying unconscious on the floor of the cage.

0:32 . . .

"No!" cried Leslie. "We've got to stop it!"

Luckily, with every ghork in the square battling against the blissfully oblivious festivalgoers, there was no one left to guard the blender. Elliot and Leslie ran to it and saw the brightly glowing control panel at its base, flashing with a single word.

PUREE . . . *PUREE* . . . *PUREE* . . .

At the bottom of the control panel, the same horrifying numbers counted down, just as they did on the view-screen above them.

0:23 . . .

Elliot reached out with his furry green finger and pressed the button marked *STOP*.

But the blender *didn't* stop. The cage kept descending toward the spinning blades. A message appeared on the control panel:

TO QUIT PURÉEING YOUR VICTIMS

PLEASE ENTER THE PASSCODE

7 8 9

4 5 6

1 2 3

0

"You didn't think it would be that easy, did you?" The Chief sat back, and his chair gave off a satisfied creak.

"Please," said Elliott. "You can't do this! It's . . . it's . . ." He couldn't think of the word awful enough to describe grinding up his friends in a giant blender. Then it came to him. "It's *abominable*!"

"It's *iniquitous*!" cried Leslie.

0:10 . . . 0:09 . . .

"I would have settled for *evil*," said the chief. He leaned forward, his teeth glittering with almost electric light. "It might be the most evil thing I've ever done. And after spoiling my plans, I hope it makes you two the saddest pair of little children in the entire universe!"

When he said this, Elliot and Leslie looked at each other.

"That's it," Elliott whispered. "The *saddest . . .*"

". . . in the *entire universe*!" cried Leslie.

0:03 . . .

Together they reached for the blender's control panel and tapped out three simple digits: 1-0-1. Instantly, the blender stopped, and (as with every deadly and dramatic countdown in history) the counter was left with just one second left.

0:01.

"Hooray!" cried the crowd of festivalgoers.

Reggie lumbered up onstage, coated in patches of lasagna and dripping with hollandaise sauce. He helped Elliot and Leslie winch the cage free of the blender. At last, they lowered it gently to the stage, where Reggie popped the lock, using his tusk like a crowbar. The bombastadon blundered inside and lifted Gügor until he was sitting up.

"Gügor, my friend, snap out of it! You've been rescued!"

"Try belching on him," suggested Bildorf.

Pib agreed. "You know what they say. Bombastadon belly gas can wake the dead!"

"Please, Colonel," said Eloise-Yvette, "if it will revive my Googy, you must!"

Reggie dutifully took a deep breath and, after a moment of stomach-rumbling, released a great *BRRRRAAAAAP*!

Gügor's face contorted in disgust, and his eyes blinked open.

Reggie clapped an arm around the knucklecrumpler's shoulders. "Gügor, old friend! Wonderful to have you back!"

"How do you feel?" Leslie asked Gügor.

"Good enough to crumple something." He leapt off the stage and led the creatures into the epic food fight. The sky whizzed with baguette arrows and pineapple artillery; the cobblestones were strewn with chili-sauce bombs and banana-peel booby traps; and the air filled with shouts of "Puddings away!" and "Incoming monkfish!"

All of this turned out to be another advantage the creatures of DENKi-3000 and the people of Simmersville had over the ghorks. After all of the Chief's wishes for a death ray (or even a "maiming ray"), it was the sheer quantity of nearby food that proved the most effective weapon against the ghorks. Each sloppy, gloppy, greasy, gooey, sticky, sludgy blow rained down on the ghorks like extreme versions of the bizarre anti-ghork devices Elliot and Leslie had invented.

Eye-ghorks were beaten with buckets of lemon juice; the hand-ghorks, with extra-slippery olive oil; the nose-ghorks, with hefty doses of Limburger and Stinking Bishop cheese; the mouth-ghorks, with tongue-lashings of chili oil; while the ear-ghorks were deafened and unbalanced with cochleas full of tenacious lard! Soon, the ghorks were running for the hills. They had finally realized how foolish it had been to attack a place like Simmersville.

Grinner shouted to the others, while frantically fanning his swollen tongue, "C'mon, everybody, let's hoof it! This town's a madhouse!"

With that, he ran off himself, leading the last remaining ghorks into the night.

"Hooray!" The Simmersville townsfolk threw up their arms, flicking food in every direction. Everyone marveled at what fun this year's cabaret had been.

"They ought to end with a food fight every year!" said one woman.

Meanwhile, up on the view-screen, the Chief realized that without his henchmen he was nothing more than a talking head. His shadowy face loomed forward, glaring down at Leslie and Elliot.

"I want you both to know," he said, "that there is nothing I hate more than being defeated by a pair of children!"

"Get used to it," said Leslie.

"*Never!*"

Then, with nothing more momentous than a fizzle of static, the Chief of Quazicom vanished.

With everyone free, Jean-Remy was able to give his sister a proper hug. They exchanged a flurry of words in French, and even though Elliot and Leslie didn't understand what they were saying they sensed the long-lost siblings had reconciled at last. Harrumphrey approached Gügor, the tip of his tail snaking up to slap the knucklecrumpler's back.

"Glad you're safe, big guy," he said.

"More important," said Patti, joining them, "have you told Eloise-Yvette how you feel?"

Gügor shook his head.

So did Patti (disappointedly). "You had all that time, locked up with her in the cage, facing certain death, *and you didn't say anything*?"

The big knucklecrumpler shrugged. "Gügor was unconscious."

"Fair point," said Patti.

Now that the Chief and his henchmen had been sent pack-ing, the only one left was Giggles. He still sat in his throne, as expressionless as ever.

Harrumphrey waddled over to the corner of the stage, Elliot and Leslie following him. "I knew it," Harrumphrey said. "From the moment I saw you up here, I *knew* we'd never get you to laugh."

"You did?" asked Leslie. "But how?"

"He's not a ghork at all," Harrumphrey told her. He turned back to the supposed Sixth Ghork. "Isn't that right?"

Giggles shook his head. "I tried to tell them it would never work," he admitted in a surprisingly deep and resonant—but decidedly expressionless—voice, "but they just wouldn't listen."

Elliot couldn't believe it. "You mean you're *not* the Fabled Sixth Ghork?"

"Not even close," Giggles admitted. "Grinner and the oth-ers told me they had looked everywhere, but couldn't find any Fabled Sixth Ghork, which is because it doesn't exist. It's kind of the same with all ancient prophecies—just a bunch of old mumbo-jumbo. But they knew if they returned empty-handed, they'd be in big trouble with their boss." He glanced up at the view-screen. "Anyway, when they found me, they said I looked ghorkish enough to pass, so they brought me back. They said all I'd have to do was sit in my throne and let them do the talking."

Leslie sighed. "So after all that, you're not even a ghork?"

Harrumphrey shook his enormous head. His tail spiraled up and gestured at Giggles. "This would be an example of creature number 902, subset B: a big-booted solemn-golem. Am I right?"

Giggles nodded. "How did you know?"

"He knows them all," Leslie explained.

"Quite a rare kind of creature," said Harrumphery. "Famous for never, *ever* laughing."

"I might," said Giggles, "if I saw something that was *actually* funny."

Out in the audience, covered with the ingredients of a hundred different dishes, two figures pushed through the crowd. It was Elliot's parents. Elliot wanted nothing more than to leap off the stage and run into their arms. But how could he, looking like this?

"Elliot?" asked his mother. "Is that *really* you?"

Elliot nodded. "It's not a costume."

"It does *sound* like you," said his father, "but . . ."

"I wish I could explain everything, but there's too much, so it'll have to wait until later. Right now all I want to say is . . . well, I'm sorry. I'm sorry I yelled at the restaurant and then ran off. I'm sorry I'm more interested in being a creature than being a food critic, and even though I know we're totally different— *especially* now—I still love you guys, and I hope you love me back, even if it means having a three-toed bristle-imp for a son."

His parents looked at each other. They still didn't seem convinced.

"Oh, wait," said Elliot. "I forgot I took it off!" He swung his knapsack off his shoulders and plucked out his bright green fishing vest.

The moment he slipped it on, his mother cried, "Elliot! It *is* you!"

Elliot felt a swell of happiness. He did just as he had wanted to moments before: He leapt off the stage and ran into his parents' arms. The crowd burst out with a collective "*Awww!*"

Even though much of this year's costume cabaret didn't make sense, a heartfelt family reunion was something they could all understand.

Onstage, however, unlike everyone else, Giggles didn't say "*Awww* . . ." He was doing something else.

He was laughing.

"*Wha-ha-ha-ha!* I'm sorry . . . but I—I—*eeee-heheheheee!*" he squealed. "I really don't mean to laugh but—*ooooh-hoh-hoh-hoh!*—but . . . but . . . a *bright green fishing vest*?! *Wha-ha-ha-ha!*"

"I don't believe it," said Leslie. She was quite shocked. "All we needed to make you laugh was in Elliot's knapsack this whole time!"

Giggles nodded vigorously, his eyes scrunched tight. It was all he could do. He was laughing too hard. "Oh, thank you," he said. "I haven't laughed this hard since . . . since . . . well, since *forever!*"

Leslie turned to her friend. "Elliot, I think I owe you an apology. I was the one who made you take off your vest, after all. If you'd been wearing it at the Great Hexposé . . ." She glanced at the enormous blender, sitting inert behind them. "We might have avoided a lot of trouble."

Elliot looked down at his vest. Was it really that funny looking? Yes, maybe it was. "I understand," he told Leslie. "You were only trying to make me look . . . cooler."

When Elliot said "cooler" Giggles laughed even louder.

Elliot tried to ignore him. "You know what I think?" he said. "Maybe coolness comes in a million different flavors." He pointed to the sloppy remnants of the food fight. "Just like food." He glanced at Giggles. "Or like humor." Finally, he pointed to

Harrumphrey. "Or like creatures!"

"Not a million," Harrumphrey corrected. "Eleven thousand—"

"Five hundred and twenty-two," Elliot finished. "*I know*. I was just trying to make a point." He rolled his eyes and took a deep breath. "What I mean is, what's cool is different for everyone. Take you, for instance. You think Boris Minor and the Karloffs are cool."

"*Hey!*" cried Boris Minor himself. "We're right here! We can hear you!"

"Well, to me," Elliot concluded, "there's nothing cooler than a bright green fishing vest!"

This time, it was Leslie's turn to find the wisdom in her friend's words. She smoothed down one of the puffier pockets on Elliot's vest. "I guess I can live with that," she said.

Elliot smiled. Watching Giggles double over with laughter, he felt more proud of his vest than ever before. "I might look like the world's dorkiest werewolf," he said, "but as long as I'm wearing my fishing vest, I know exactly who I am!"

"You're our son," said Elliot's father, squeezing him tightly. "And we don't care *what* you look like, we'll always love you."

Elliot's mother squeezed him even harder. "You'll always be our Elliot."

"That's good to hear," said Elliot, "because, like the other specimens here . . ."—he pointed to the edge of the stage, where Emily and the others stood in a nervous huddle—"there's no way to turn us back."

"I wouldn't be so sure about that!" called a voice.

It was an old voice with a crackle in every word, and it had come from the entranceway of the Simmersville Inn. It was a voice Leslie recognized.

IGLOO GLUE
9000

CHAPTER 28

In which Leslie learns some family history, and Elliot learns
that there's a little creature in everyone

randpa Freddy!" cried Leslie.

When she looked toward the hotel, however, she
saw that it wasn't him. It wasn't even a human. It was
a creature, the same one Elliot and Leslie had seen when they first
arrived. It was the thing from the hotel's aquarium, the sea creature that was part turtle, part lobster, part starfish.

In spite of its oddness, there was something charming in the
clumsy way it hobbled and slapped across the market square.
(One of the astonished onlookers commented, "That is *definitely*
the best costume of all!") Stranger still, the creature was dressed
in chef's whites and carried a tray with a silver dome on top.

With everyone stunned into silence, the creature toddled and
slithered onstage. He lifted the silver-domed platter. Underneath
were two things: a bamboo box, just like the ones in which
dumplings were served at Leslie's restaurant, and a clear glass
bottle, filled with a reddish-pink fluid.

Leslie pointed to the bottle. "That looks like . . ."

Before she could finish, the creature unscrewed the corkscrewed, and Leslie caught a whiff of something familiar, a peculiar

scent of honey, pickled plums, and Worcestershire sauce.

"*It is!* That's Grandpa Freddy's cooking wine!" Leslie looked into the creature's tortoise-like face. "What are you going to do with that?"

"The same thing I've been doing ever since I first laid eyes on your grandmother." With three great gulps, the creature drained the bottle. Even before the last swallow had rumpled the loose and leathery skin of his neck, a miraculous transformation had begun.

Before everyone's eyes, the turtle shell shrank and lost all its color. It became a kind of external spine, but the chain of vertebrae were only visible for a moment. They were sucked inside the creature's newly soft (and newly pink) skin. Next, the creature's arms and legs lost their orange color and pebbled surface. Every appendage withered to become the limbs of a lean and wrinkly human being.

"Grandpa Freddy! I knew you couldn't let the Food Festival pass by without coming, but . . . but . . ." Leslie didn't know what to say. Her happiness at finding her grandfather was over-shadowed by what she had just witnessed.

Meanwhile, Leslie's mother was stalking over from her stall in the market square, dripping with the remnants of the food fight. "*Dad?* Is that really you?"

"In the flesh," said Famous Freddy.

"But how? *And why?*"

"The same reason we all do foolish things," said Leslie's grandfather. "Because I was in love. When I saw your mother, I wanted nothing more than to be with her, so I cooked up a potion to disguise myself as a human being."

Leslie's mother gripped the edge of the stage to steady herself, perhaps to keep herself from fainting. "Are you saying you *tricked* Mom into marrying you?"

Grandpa Freddy laughed. "Of course not! Your mother knew the truth about me long before we were married. I was so nervous to show her who I really was, but she still loved me when I finally did." He turned to Elliot. "Just like you and your parents."

Leslie picked the empty bottle off the tray. "So *that's* why you were always drinking this stuff at the restaurant. Your 'cooking wine.' I always thought you were a drunk!"

"No, just a creature."

In her head, Leslie tried to decide which was worse. Then something occurred to her. "But that means . . . *I'm* part creature, too?"

Elliot climbed back onstage and put one hairy hand on his friend's shoulder. "I'm beginning to think there's a little creature in all of us." He smiled weakly at Famous Freddy and then looked down at his hairy bristle-imp body. "Sometimes, a little *too much.*"

"Don't you worry," said Leslie's grandfather. "I've got just the thing for that."

"You do?"

Famous Freddy nodded. "Dr. Benedict Heppleworth is an old friend. He called me here when Quazicom took over. That was why I left in such a hurry. In my natural form as a creature I was able to hide myself—in that huge aquarium at the Simmersville Inn."

"So you were there all along," said Elliot. "You saw us eating when we first arrived."

"It's not all I saw. I was keeping an eye on Grinner in the

kitchen. I needed to see what went into that 'Special' he served you. So I was able to cook up an antidote using all the same ingredients." He lifted the lid on the bamboo box sitting on the tray. Inside was a dainty ring of six steamed dumplings.

He handed Elliot a pair of chopsticks and said, "That one's for you."

Elliot stared at the dumpling.

"And these," Famous Freddy said to the others, "are for you."

The other "Specimens" shuffled onto the stage: the creature like a bright red polar bear; the businessman with the head of a giraffe; the four-armed troll; the one-eyed, mostly belly creature; and Emily, the shimmering green lizard. Freddy gave them each a dumpling, and when they ate it, a miraculous transformation occurred. All five of them were human once again!

"Oh, thank you, thank you!" Emily cried. She gave Famous Freddy a big hug. "If there's ever anything I can do to repay you, you just let me know!"

Leslie's grandfather shook his head. "Don't mention it. Just make sure the next time you visit Bickleburgh, you stop in for a bite at Famous Freddy's Dim Sum Emporium!"

Elliot peered into the bamboo box. "There's only one left," he said.

"It's for you," said Famous Freddy.

Elliot was about to reach for it with his chopsticks, when he stopped. "But what about the snooty waiter?"

"What waiter?" asked Leslie's grandfather.

Elliot explained how the ghorks had tested their formula on the man—and how it had worked.

"I could certainly try and whip something up," said the old chef, "but where is he?"

Elliot, Leslie and the creatures looked around the market square but (thankfully) there wasn't a ghork in sight.

"Poor guy," said Leslie. "I hope he's okay . . . wherever he is."

Famous Freddy squeezed Elliot's shoulder and pointed at the final remaining dumpling. "Like I said, that one's for you."

As he poked his chopsticks into the box, Elliot's head filled with a whirl of questions. Did he *really* want to go back to his old self? Hadn't his parents accepted him as a creature only a moment ago? And wasn't this what he had always wanted? To belong to the world of his uncle Archie, to the world of creatures?

Yes . . .

Except . . .

Deep down, he knew the truth. As much as he loved creaturedom, he wasn't truly a creature himself—at least not on the *outside*. Now that he knew his parents would accept him no matter what, he knew precisely where he belonged.

He plucked up Famous Freddy's dumpling and popped it into his mouth.

It tasted a bit strange, but as with all of Freddy's cooking, it was delicious.

He swallowed.

He waited.

At first, nothing happened, but then Elliot felt very strange. A warm, tingling sensation prickled all through his body. The bristling, hedgehog-like hair was sucked into his skin. His eyes lost their yellow tint. His wolfish snout shrunk and vanished, as did his long, shining talons. In seconds, Elliot was back to his old self. But at the same time, he knew he would always be a creature—at least on the *inside*.

The crowd cheered. They had never seen anything like it.

Many of them would remember these transformations as the greatest quick-change illusions they had ever seen (it was simply too much for them to believe it was real).

Gügor lumbered over to Elliot and put one great arm around his shoulders. "Thank you," he said.

"Watch it," Elliot responded. "I'm getting crumpled down here! *Wait*. Thank you—for what?"

"Not you. Them." Gügor was pointing to Elliot's parents. "And you." Gügor pointed to Famous Freddy.

"You're welcome," said Leslie's grandfather. "But why?"

"Because Elliot's parents would love Elliot no matter what he looked like, and because Grandpa Freddy loved Grandma Freddy even though she was different from him. If love can happen between such different people then maybe it can also happen between . . . you know."

"This is it," Patti whispered to Harrumphrey. "He's finally gonna tell her!"

Gügor turned to Eloise-Yvette. "Gügor knows," he said, "that Eloise-Yvette is very different from Gügor. Mostly, it's a difference of size. Gügor doesn't think this is a problem. So Gügor wants to say: Eloise-Yvette Chevalier, you are, and have always been, Gügor's 1TL."

Patti cupped one hand to her mouth and turned to the audience. "That means *One True Love*," she whispered.

"Oh, Googy," said Eloise-Yvette. "Why would I find that strange?"

"Gügor and Eloise-Yvette are so different."

As Gügor said this, the lights in the market square dimmed. (This was because the lighting crew, who, like the audience, sensed the romantic climax of the show, thought a bit of mood lighting was called for.) It seemed as though the whole world dimmed, save for a single spotlight. It lanced across the square to hit upon Gügor and Eloise-Yvette, whose wings sparkled like the stars.

"Of course I don't think it's strange." she said. "I'm a *fairy-bat*, silly! If there's one kind of creature in all of creaturedom who understands the possibility of love between mismatched couples, it's us fairy-bats! But Gooey, that's not the only reason I think it's perfectly normal." She flew to Gügor's face and cupped his enormous chin inside her tiny hand. "When I saw you break your chains and fight single-handed against an army of ghorks to save me, I knew it was true. It made me realize something I should have realized all those years ago, when we sang together in the catacombs."

"What was that?" asked Gügor.

Eloise-Yvette fluttered forward and gave him a great big (well, "great big" by fairy-bat standards, which was actually minuscule by knucklecrumpler standards, but . . . well, you get the picture) kiss.

"You're not my brother," she said. "You're my ITL."

"*Aww!*" went the crowd (the second time) followed by thunderous applause. In fact, Eloise-Yvette's kiss received a standing ovation.

"I'd say this calls for a song," said Boris Minor. "Anybody feel like cutting us down?"

Boris and the band took to the stage and played a funky backup to a duet from Gügor and Eloise-Yvette. First, Eloise-Yvette sang:

After sunset, strolling home

Empty streets, I'm all alone.
The sky is deep and full of stars.
There's nothing like this feeling.

Then came Gügor's deep, drawling voice:

Beneath a city no one sees
Shadows feel like friends to me.
The earth is deep and full of life
My heart could do with healing.

And at last, in harmony:

We'll have it all, the Earth and sky
When we're together, you and I . . .

"*Yick*," said Leslie, off on the edge of the stage. "Who would've thought Gügor was such a sap!"

"I know." Harrumphrey sniffled. "Such a beautiful song!"

Elliot raised his eyebrows. "Are you *crying*?"

The fluffy end of Harrumphrey's tail whipped up to dab at his cheek. "You gotta admit," he blubbered, "there's a *whole lotta love* in the square tonight!"

It was true. Everyone could feel it: Elliot's parents, who hugged each other and swayed to the music; the professor, Leslie's mother, and Famous Freddy; Patti, Harrumphrey, and Cosmo Clutch; Reggie, Bildorf, and Pib; Boris Minor and each of the Karloffs; and the whole crowd of festivalgoers, all of them dripping with what had once been their dinners, who had come to the Simmersville Food Festival and witnessed the single finest example of dinner-theatre-style costume cabaret ever performed. All of them could feel the love.

All but one.

There was one person—or rather, *creature*—who felt nothing but loneliness.

"*No!*" cried Jean-Remy, covering his heart with his hand. "Bernard! Bernard, it is too much!"

"Who's Bernard?" asked the festival emcee.

"All of zees love!" cried Jean-Remy. "I cannot take it! I *must* find her!" Having shouted this for all to hear, he leapt up and soared into the sky.

"Jean-Remy?" asked Gügor. "Where are you going?"

But the fairy-bat was too high to hear.

"I think," said Eloise-Yvette, "he has gone to find his fairy princess."

"Hard to blame him," said Patti, "what with all the love in the square."

"Do you think he'll find her?" asked Leslie.

Eloise-Yvette raised her face, searching the sky for her brother. "Yes," she said at last, "I have a feeling he will."

Everyone else looked up, too, hoping to see a glimmer from the fairy-bat's pearlescent wings. But Jean-Remy was gone. All they saw was the sparkle of the stars.

ACKNOWLEDGMENTS

My deepest gratitude to the many people involved in bringing this second Creature Department book to life: My publisher, Ben Schrank, and my editor, Rebecca Kilman, at Razorbill/Penguin in New York; Jackie Kaiser at Westwood Creative Artists in Toronto; Nick Hooker, Mike Woods, and Meg Diamond at Framestore New York; Simon Whalley, Selena Stokes, and the digital team at Framestore London (who granted me the distinct pleasure of an edifying chat with Gügor); and of course, last but not least, a great knucklecrumpler round of applause for Zack Lydon, the illustrator behind the book's eye-popping artwork.